D1267981

AN ECHO OF THE FAE

JENELLE LEANNE SCHMIDT

DEDICATION

For the sparrows, and those who love them.
Though flown from our arms, forever in our hearts.

PROLOGUE

DREAMS AND MEMORIES

*M*y earliest memory returns often in my dreams. My mother's soft smile caresses me as she bends down to kiss my forehead, my own tiny hand reaching up and trying to capture a lock of her long red-gold hair between clumsy fingers that refuse to obey my wish. A soft, sweet humming fills the memory, a tune that is both dear and yet unfamiliar. Eyes filled with love gaze down at me, and a gentle laugh, a man's laugh, fills the room. Strong arms encircle us both, my mother and me, and I know I am perfectly safe. Perfectly loved.

Another sound permeates the memory: a rhythmic, rushing, liquid sound I do not recognize, but which fills me with a deep longing that threatens to burst out of my chest and leave me completely hollow. In the dream, it is merely a subtle noise in the background, but when I wake I feel a desperate need to find its source. Sometimes the longing clutches me so tightly that it leaves me gasping, desperately sucking in each breath as if through a narrow reed, my lungs screaming as though they have forgotten how to breathe the very air I need to survive.

It is rare to have a memory from such a tender age, especially one so vivid. And yet, that moment is locked in my thoughts with perfect clarity. During the day it grows distant and faded, but it has haunted my sleep in full, vibrant detail each night for nearly thirteen years.

So why is it that the face in my dreams is wholly unfamiliar to me? Why is the mother from my memory a stranger?

ECHOES OF FEAR

*E*cho sat on a salt-smoothed boulder, her knees pulled up to her chin, watching the other village children playing along the beach. Some of them traversed the shore collecting shells in wicker baskets. The braver ones waded out into the water, splashing and swimming in the gently rolling waves. A shudder coursed through her. Even if it were not early spring and the waters were warmer, nothing would induce her to go any closer to that surging surf and those unfathomable depths. Who knew what untold terrors the placidly sparkling surface concealed?

A cluster of girls stood in the wet sand where the waves lapped about their ankles, baskets swinging from their arms, the foaming water swirling at their feet. She imagined ghostly, watery hands reaching out to capture them, pulling them beneath the surface, deeper and deeper until all memory of light and warmth was long forgotten.

A flurry of laughter pulled her out of her dark thoughts and she noticed one of them—a tiny, dark-haired girl named Branna—waving to her. Echo narrowed her eyes. She and

Branna had been friends as children, but their friendly inter-actions had ended abruptly one day when a group of chil-dren had gathered around Echo in the school yard, teasing her about her love of the forest, mocking her elfin looks, and calling her a "faeling." One of the boys had loudly pointed out how Echo looked nothing like either of her parents, and so she must be a changeling, sent to cause bad luck on the family and the village. "Echo of the Fae!" he had accused, and the other children had taken up his words, turning them into a taunting chant as they circled around her.

Echo vividly remembered looking to her playmate for help, and finding none. Branna had not joined in the teasing, but she had done nothing to defend Echo, either. Their friendship died in that moment. And though Branna had made a few overtures after that, Echo could not let go of her grudge.

Echo's family was highly regarded by the other villagers. Gerard McIntyre had helped found Ennis Rosliath, which gave the McIntyres a respectable standing in the community. Runa McIntyre, Echo's mother, was beloved as much for her kindness as for her medicinal herbs and delicious baked goods. And Gareth, Echo's father, was esteemed, though rumors still swirled about his accident at sea and his miracu-lous return.

Echo herself was smiled at by the adults who patted her head awkwardly, and generally ignored by their children. Friendship might have been extended, if Echo had been able to forgive the taunts and cruel teasing, but she struggled to trust their intentions. Especially when she heard the word "faeling" muttered in groups and saw their disdainful glances tossed her way when school was in session. And even if she could have found the strength to let go of her grudges, something else held Echo back. Her mother called it shyness, and perhaps that was it. That strangling sensation that started in her middle and crept up her body to lodge in her temples with a thudding, throbbing beat that drowned out her ability to think of anything to say or ask. When she did find words, they came out garbled or backwards. Any attempt to be part of the group ended in embarrassment, her ears burning as she scrambled for some pretense to excuse herself.

Branna was still looking her way. The other girl took a hesitant step toward Echo, but one of her friends grabbed her arm and pointed and they all dashed off down the beach, squealing over a particularly good trove of shells. Echo watched them go, a pang flitting through her.

Echo wrapped her arms around herself and shivered in the sunshine. Although spring was well on its way, the air still held a nip of winter. The breeze coming off the water threw a light mist against her skin, and the droplets were like the icy kisses of snowflakes on her bare arms.

She glanced up at the promontory that bounded the beach where her house stuck up from the headland like a proud piece of driftwood carried onto the sands. Hadn't she fulfilled Mamai's wishes by coming down to the shore? Surely she had not intended for her to spend the entire afternoon on the beach? Echo waffled in her own mind, torn between the desire to please her mother and her own discomfort at being so near to the ocean and the waves that heaved themselves hungrily onto the shore, ever closer to the rock she had chosen as her refuge.

The signs of the rising tide settled the decision for her. Echo leaped from her spot and set off at as sedate a pace as she could manage. When she crested the hill she paused, drinking in the emerald hues of pastureland spreading out across the valley that separated her from the village to the east. A breath of wind brushed her face, bringing with it the scent of earth and trees. Her pulse quickened as the breeze ruffled her loose hair, teasing her with its playfulness. She began to run. She did not run east toward the village, nor did her feet take her west, out onto the promontory toward home. No, the wildness she felt in the wind called her north, to the Faeorn.

The great, old forest that stretched across the heart of Ennis Rosliath had the distinguished mark of being Echo's favorite place on the island. The ancient giants towered above her, inviting her to climb up and explore their heights. Leafy ferns and soft pine needles covered its floor, muting the scampering feet and fluttering wings that inhabited it. Here, she did not have to navigate the awkward conventions of socializing. It did not matter to the forest inhabitants that she had delicate features that bore no resemblance to either of her parents. Here, she could bask in the assurance of remaining undisturbed.

The people of Ennis Rosliath went out of their way to avoid the Faeorn, cradle of many of the island's midnight tales. Cunning sprites and vindictive ghosts were the least of its rumors. On occasion, a brave or desperate soul might harvest the timber on its outskirts, but this was never lightly done. For every tree chopped down for fuel, two more were planted in its place so as not to incite the forest's wrath. And if the person who needed the wood did not have the money for such an offering, the rest of the townspeople would unite to cover the cost. A few gyeads were considered a small price to pay to ward off the ire of any malevolent forest spirits.

Echo did not fear the forest or its supposed spirits. She had never found anything but peace and quiet joy within the dappled woods. Within its cool embrace she had made friends who were unbothered by her long silences or her terror of the ocean that her neighbors revered as protector and provider. None of these friends ever teased her. Here in the depths of the forest, Echo felt at home as she did nowhere else. Sometimes, within the cool paths of the greenwood, Echo did feel as though eyes were upon her, but it was not an ominous sensation—more like a watchful, guarding presence, like the gaze of her parents before they trusted her to walk into town alone.

With a faint sigh of relief, she settled herself in between the roots of a great oak, her back resting against its trunk. She leaned her head back, studying the mesmerizing patterns in the leaves above, relishing the way the green foliage captured and redirected beams of sunlight, transforming golden rays into a soft, verdant glow that bathed the forest below. She sat quietly, unmoving. Waiting. A tiny rustle drifted to her ears, but she did not turn. Instead, she slowly reached into the small bag hanging from her shoulder and pulled out the treats she had packed to share with her friends. A sliver of guilt pierced her thoughts. Even as she had prepared to go down to the beach like Mamai wanted, she had known she would end up here instead. She dug for a handful of seeds and scattered them about.

"I try, really, I do," she whispered as a squirrel scampered along the root near her foot. She broke off a portion of her honey cake and set it on the ground, nibbling on a corner of the piece she kept for herself, its crumbly sweetness doing little to assuage the sudden melancholy that assailed her. "They always look like they're having so much fun, splashing around. I wish I could join them, but... I can't. I just can't. What is wrong with me? I haven't always been so scared."

It was true. Though she had never loved the ocean, she had not always been frightened by it. The terror had grown slowly, though she could remember the day it had begun.

SHE HAD BEEN JUST six years old, playing on the rocks that jutted from the shore near the base of the cliffs below their house. She bounded from one outcropping to another, until she found one with an interesting depression in it, full of water. She crouched down to inspect the shells and the tiny fish that darted about within, trapped until the next tide. After a while, when the water started lapping at her feet, she looked up and realized her perch was surrounded. The waves had quietly crept past her while she played. Panic gripped her, and she screamed, long and loud.

Her father came running, splashing through the waves—which barely covered his knees—and lifted her off the rock. He placed her on his shoulders and forged through the swirling water back to the safety of the shore, where he put her down and gently reprimanded her for neglecting awareness of the tides.

She trotted along behind him as he retrieved a bucket of fish he had been carrying, which he took out onto a rocky outcropping and shook out into the water.

"Are you leaving an offering for the sea god, Dadai?" she asked.

He knelt down and placed his hands on her shoulders. "Echo, I want you to listen carefully. There is only one God, the Creator, who reigns over all things."

"Then why does everyone else throw things into the sea?" she asked, puzzled.

Dadai sighed. "Do you know the little stick puppets I made to help me tell stories sometimes?"

Echo nodded enthusiastically. She loved those puppets, and the way her Dadai gave them different voices as he acted out Bible stories and tales from his other storybooks.

"Well, what if I could bring them to life?"

Echo's eyes widened at the prospect.

Dadai smiled. "What if I gave them everything they needed, taught them how to talk, how to walk, how to fish and climb trees and"—he tugged playfully on her pigtail—"even braid hair."

She giggled. "That would be fun."

"Yes, it would. But then what if, even though I created those little puppets and poured my own breath and heart and blood into them, they decided I wasn't all that important? What if they decided to make their own little stick puppet and pretend that it made them? Or what if they decided to follow... Mamai's rocking chair? What if they decided I didn't even exist?"

Echo stomped her little foot at this. "That... that..." She searched for strong enough words for this imaginary turn of events. "That would be vicious disgrateful of them!" she finally exclaimed.

Dadai did not laugh at her fury. Instead he nodded soberly. "That it would. And yet, that is what it is like for many people. They'd rather follow something they made up."

"Why?"

"Because it lets them pretend to be masters of their own lives and gives them permission to listen only to themselves."

Echo thought about that for a moment. She scrunched up her face. "Is the bucket of fish for the Creator God, then?"

At that, Dadai laughed and rose. "No, little wood-sprite."

"Then why?"

Instead of answering, Dadai put a finger to his lips and crouched back down. "Look!" he whispered, pointing out to sea.

As Echo watched, a pod of seals surfaced, their smooth heads breaking through the surface of the waves. They splashed about, bobbing up and diving down after the fish. Then they began to approach the shore, and Echo held her breath. She watched them with her father as they came nearer, up onto the rocks, almost close enough for her to touch. She longed to stroke their silky fur, but instead she held perfectly still, barely daring to blink lest she frighten them away. Their ungainly movements and deep, liquid eyes were strange and alien, but she was enchanted nonetheless. Her father was silent, somehow solemn, and neither of them spoke for a long while. But eventually, one of the seals gave a short, sharp bark, and then the pod disappeared back into the water, leaving behind only sparkling ripples and a few stray fish bones.

THE SQUIRREL CHITTERED AT ECHO, breaking her reminiscence. His tail flicked twice and he gazed at her over the bit of honey cake. Echo started to whisper back, but their conversation was disrupted by a few crossbills fluttering down and alighting near her feet. They hopped about, pecking at her offering of seeds and ruffling their colorful feathers. She smiled, then turned at a disturbance in the undergrowth and saw a small bunny poke its head out from beneath a large, leafy fern, its nose wiggling curiously. Echo laid down the cabbage leaf that had contained the honey cakes and the rabbit came forward and nibbled appreciatively. On graceful legs, a doe emerged from between the trees, eyes wary and proud, ears flicking attentively as its young fawn peeked out from behind her.

In hushed delight, Echo held out a few lumps of salt. "Hello, new little one."

The doe leaned her head down gracefully, lipping at the salt, but the fawn merely stared at her with wide, frightened eyes.

"There's no need to be afraid," Echo said to it, "but I understand being shy of strangers."

When the doe had thoroughly cleaned her hand, Echo leaned back and stared up at the specks of azure sky peeking through the canopy. The other animals finished the meal she had brought them and gazed at her, but when no more food was forthcoming, they began to wander off in search of other sources of sustenance.

Echo stood and picked her way through the forest, finding one of the numerous deer trails and following it through the underbrush, ducking her head and plowing through the thicker tangles. Eventually, she found her way out of the trail into a clearing surrounded by willow trees. Grinning in delight, she grabbed a handful of the long, leafy branches and, with a running leap, swung across the ground. Her bare toes stretched out and kicked off the trunk, sending her swinging backwards again. She giggled at the rush of air and freedom she felt.

When she grew tired of swinging, she pushed aside the long, green willow branches and settled herself inside the tree's natural curtain. Pulling her small knife from her bag, she picked up a piece of wood and began carefully carving a notch at one end with some idea of making a whistle. She worked methodically, her fingers clumsy at the task, her dark head bent over the branch. The first one did not turn out well, so she tried again, this time with better results. At least, the second whistle made some noise when she blew upon it.

"This is so much better than going wading," she murmured. "If only Mamai understood."

Her conscience scolded even as the words left her mouth. Mamai tried to understand. Echo knew this in the depths of her bones. It was an inescapable tension between them, though, for as much as Echo feared the sea, Mamai loved it. Echo had often seen her pause in a task and stare out at the glistening waves, her face alight with such a fiery passion it almost scared her to look at it.

A frisson of remembered fear zipped across the backs of her hands, making them tense, clutching at the folds of her skirt and jerking it up, frightening the wildlife around her. The crossbills flapped away and the squirrel raced up a nearby trunk, scolding her all the way. Echo barely noticed.

SHE HAD BARELY BEEN MORE than a toddler, but that memory was more vivid and made her heart race more surely than even being stranded by the tides. That wild, windy day when the sea was restless and she saw that look on her mother's face for the first time.

The huge, hungry waves were crashing against the rocks beneath their house in a rhythmic drumbeat while they picked raspberries on the bluff. Echo had pricked her finger on a vine and looked up for some sympathy, but her mother was not in sight. Panic surged through her as she stumbled to her feet, toddling around the corner of her house, where she saw her mother standing transfixed, facing the point of the peninsula and the sea below. The wind whipped her dress about and her long auburn hair streamed out behind her. The intensity of the coming storm was mirrored in the wild joy on her face and Echo, young as she was, could almost feel her mother's strange longing like a tangible thing.

"Mamai!" she had cried, running, stumbling, tripping across the rocky ground to grasp hold of her mother's skirts. Tears streaming down her face, Echo had choked and sobbed into the rough woolen fabric. "Mamai, don't leave me!"

Strong, comforting arms had swept her off the ground, and Mamai pressed her forehead against hers for a long moment. Then she pulled back a bit, her soft brown eyes gazing into Echo's. She knew she would never forget that moment for as long as she lived: that mixture of agony and sorrow and love in Mamai's gaze. Her mother had squeezed her tightly.

"Never, my darling," she had whispered the promise. "I will never leave you, my Echo."

2

THE CONFESSION

*I*n the silver mist of a cloudy twilight, Echo made her way home. She let herself in through the front door, guilt weighing like a heavy stone in the pit of her stomach. Mamai stood over the stove, her hair wrapped around her head in a crown of messy braids, with wisps sticking out all around her face. When she heard the door, she turned, a warm smile on her face.

"Echo!" She greeted her with a floury hug. "Did you have a nice time?"

Self-reproach burbled within her, and Echo hung her head, unable to meet her mother's inquisitive gaze.

"You didn't go to the seaside, did you?" The weariness in Mamai's voice broke something inside Echo, and she buried her head in her mother's shoulder.

"I did! I tried!" she exclaimed. Then she pushed herself away, her eyes fixed on the floorboards under her bare feet. Suddenly, the words she had never before been able to say began to tumble out of her mouth unbidden. "But I couldn't stay. I don't belong there, Mamai! No matter how much I try,

I can't... the waves... I know you love the ocean, and for you... I try to love it, too, but..." Echo gulped, choking on a half-formed sob. "It terrifies me. I always feel like the waves are reaching for me, waiting to pull me under and never let me go." Echo clamped her lips shut, aghast and wishing she could take the words back. A long silence stretched out between them, until Echo could bear it no longer. "I did try, Mamai," she whispered. Though she felt she would crumble to dust to see the hurt there, she could not help but risk a quick glance up into her mother's eyes. Her gaze caught and held, and amazement stirred in Echo's soul, for she saw no disappointment in her mother's face; instead, there was only tender compassion.

"My Echo." Mamai's arms wrapped around her shoulders and Echo felt all her defenses collapse. "Why haven't you told me before that you're afraid of the ocean?"

"I..." Echo shrugged, uncomfortable. "I guess I thought you knew and just wanted me to get over it."

"I knew you didn't like to swim there, but you love playing in the river so... it never occurred to me that you might be scared."

"I'm sorry," Echo mumbled. "It's just... I know how much you love the ocean." Mamai's eyebrows shot up. "I can see it in your face. Especially on stormy days, or when the weather changes and the waves are bigger. I wanted to love it, too. For you. I thought if you knew, you'd..."

"Oh, sweetheart." Mamai shook her head and pursed her lips, then heaved a sigh. "Echo McIntyre. I have never heard such foolishness in all my life. There are things that are important in this world, and things that aren't. Having different likes and dislikes than someone else is one of those things that aren't. If we all liked the same thing"—Mamai threw her arms out to either side in a grand gesture—"well, this would be a pretty boring world to live in, don't you think? What use would we have for tellers of tales or singers of songs? What use would we have for artisans of any kind if we all liked the exact same stories, the same colors, and the same patterns? You, my dear child, are more than welcome to have your own tastes." Mamai lowered her arms and a look of horror spread over her face. "Supper!" she exclaimed and whirled back to the stove. There was a hasty check to see that neither soup nor bread had burned, then she glanced over her shoulder, her expression gentling. "Now, you set the table and tell me about your day. You might not have stayed long at the ocean, but from the look in your eyes and the roses in your cheeks I can tell you enjoyed yourself. I think it's high time I learned about the things my daughter loves."

Echo set plates on the small table and filled three glasses with fresh, cold well water as she told her mother about her special haven in the Faeorn and the animal friends she had made there.

"Of course I don't mind you going into the Faeorn." Runa smiled as Echo finished setting out the silverware. "But in the future, please tell me when you go. And..." A shadow passed over her face. "Just... be careful you don't go too far. The forest itself is not as dangerous as the villagers believe, but there are things..." She hesitated.

Echo frowned. Her fearless mother sounded genuinely apprehensive. "Mamai?"

Mamai gave herself a little shake. "Just... promise me you will be wary of strangers, inside and outside the Faeorn."

"Of course!" Echo declared. But a niggle of worry shivered through her thoughts. Was there something to fear within the forest? Her parents were not superstitious, and had always waved away the stories about Faeorn being haunted. But, Echo suddenly realized, as far as she knew, they had never crossed its borders, either. Could there be some truth to the stories after all?

So focused was she on the shadows in her mother's eyes that Echo jumped and let out half a scream when the front door opened. She came down breathless, but then flung herself at the figure silhouetted there.

"Dadai!" she shouted.

"My little wood-sprite!" he roared, wrapping his arms around her and spinning her around so quickly her feet flew off the floor. Laughing, he set her down and crossed the kitchen to give Mamai a kiss. "Something smells delicious," he said.

"After spending all day on the docks with nothing but those smelly nets to keep you company, just about anything would smell delicious," Mamai teased, swatting him with a towel as he tried to pluck a vegetable out of her frying pan.

"Ah! Runa! Can ye not see that I am famished?" Dadai threw himself to one knee in a dramatic pose. "Have mercy on me, sweet Runa!"

Mamai laughed. "Go an' get washed up fer dinner, both of ye!" She said, affecting a deep accent as she played along with Dadai's game. "Supper'll be ready by the time ye return. Dinna worry, ye'll not faint of hunger afore then."

Dadai rose to his feet, grinning. With a wild look in his eye he swooped his arms around Mamai and kissed her soundly. Before she could recover, he released her and plucked a slice of yellow squash from the frying pan, darting quickly out of reach of her towel, a sparkle of mischief in his green eyes.

"Gareth!" Mamai spluttered, but Echo grinned, knowing that the outrage was purely for show.

"Come along, me wood-sprite." Dadai looped his arm through Echo's. "The queen of the kitchen demands cleanliness before her table, and we her humble servants must obey, must we not?"

Laughing, they ran out to the pump together, where they splashed each other, and more incidentally, their hands and faces before returning to the cottage. When they were all seated, Dadai gave the nightly thanks to the Creator, and then they set to the savory meal.

As they ate, Dadai regaled them with the strange and ridiculous things he had witnessed on the docks that day. Echo and her mother laughed uproariously as he did various impressions of the sailors and the other fishermen.

Echo knew that her father loved the open ocean every bit as much as Mamai, but an accident long ago had stolen its wonders from him and still grieved his heart. No longer fit to be a sailor himself, he worked hard at the docks, getting as close to the waves and the ships as he could, but the strenuous, drudging work of a stevedore had long since scrubbed away whatever dreams he had left of adventure and exploration. It was doubly hard recently because times had been lean for a while, which made everyone a bit testy—though Dadai always managed to portray the frustrated bickering of the other men down at the docks in a humorous light. Echo hugged her knees and felt the warmth of admiration glowing steady in her heart. Even after the most difficult day, he always managed to come home and make his family laugh.

When the meal was finished and the pots were scrubbed and hanging up to dry, Dadai moved to his favorite arm chair by the hearth and opened a large book. Echo grinned and grabbed a quilt, curling up with her back to the stones, her eyes fixed on her father's face. Mamai settled down in her rocking chair, gathering up her basket of yarn. It was Echo's favorite time of day—this time in the quiet of the evening when Dadai read to them. Sometimes it was from his beloved and much-battered Bible, though that was more often their morning fare. Evenings were for adventures— great heroes, high stakes, and daring feats. Dadai owned less than two dozen books—still more than anyone else on the island—but he treasured each volume of his small library.

As he rifled through the pages, looking for where he had left off the night before, he leaned forward and rubbed his knee. Echo winced sympathetically; she knew that when a storm was imminent, it often pained him. That accident— and the story behind it—had become a legend in Ennis Rosliath.

In his youth, some years before he'd married Mamai, her father had been on watch in the crow's nest when his ship was struck by lightning. The rest of the crew saw the splintered remains of the mast crash beneath the waves, taking Gareth down with it; they had searched for him, but in the dark and grueling tempest, they could find no trace. However, nearly three months later, Gareth McIntyre had materialized on the rocky outcropping of the northern shore, his only lasting injury a miraculously unbroken, but still grievously damaged, left knee.

The rest of the islanders said he had bested the sea god in a game of riddles, or won back his life from Death in a test of cunning or strength. Echo had always assumed that an angel had saved him like the one God had sent to close the lions' mouths to rescue Daniel. But Dadai himself had never spoken about how he survived.

He looked up from the book, his hand pausing.

"Storm tonight," he said.

A strange, knowing look passed between him and Runa. Echo frowned, suddenly realizing that she had witnessed this same exchange a hundred times before and never thought anything of it. But suddenly it struck her as odd. Her father's words, like a ritual, ignited an eager spark in Mamai's eyes as she glanced toward the window, as though expecting a sudden lightning strike. A long pause, and then the moment was gone, replaced by the click of Mamai's knitting needles and Dadai's strong voice taking on a familiar cadence as he launched into Odysseus's encounter with the sirens. Echo blinked, wondering if she had imagined the entire exchange. But no, Mamai's eyes flicked to the door, her expression taut and expectant. It was most confusing and caused a flutter of unease in her stomach. But Dadai's voice overrode the unsettling sensation, pulling her into the story and setting her imagination adrift as she sailed through tempest and peril with one of her favorite characters. By the time he finished, the strangeness of the moment was all but forgotten. With a sleepy smile, Echo embraced her parents and climbed the ladder to her loft room where she fell into bed, exhausted.

3

A STORMY NIGHT

*S*leep refused to come. First her side ached and she turned fitfully on her bed, but that made her covers twist oddly and then she had to sit up and rearrange everything before lying back down. Then her mind whirled through her experiences of the day and dreams for tomorrow, useless ramblings in her mind that she could not quiet. Her heart thudded expectantly, as though she were waiting for something. The crackle of the fire in the hearth, the sound of her mother's rocker thumping slowly and rhythmically, the indistinct murmurs of her parents' voices—these lullaby sounds drifted up through the floorboards of her loft even now, but this night, something had changed. She caught herself straining her ears, listening for something different, something more, but what, she could not have said.

Eventually, she must have dozed, because she suddenly found herself startled and disoriented. Echo blinked up at the dark rafters just above her head, wondering what had woken her, when it came again: a distant rumble of thunder. At that moment, she came fully awake, realizing that this was the sound she had been waiting for; this, the storm her father had foretold.

The patter of rain began to sound on the roof, tapping out an ominous rhythm that caused her breath to quicken and her heart to pound in her ears. A flash of light, and then a crashing boom that shook the cottage with its force. Echo pulled her blanket up over her face, clutching at it with both hands like a small child. Slowly, she peeked out, wondering what portent lay in her heart at the approach of the storm. She had never feared storms before, and yet this one filled her with such dread she felt she might fly apart at the seams.

She lay still, listening. All was quiet in the house below. Or was it? A voice filtered through the hammering rain—Dadai's deep rumble, and then Mamai's treble answered, though Echo could not make out the words. Another rumble of thunder, and beneath its rolling bass, she could just pick out the higher-pitched creak of the front door opening.

Quietly, so as not to alert her parents, Echo crept out of her bed, dragging her quilt with her, and tiptoed to her window that looked out over the front of the house. Before the open front door, she could make out a faint rectangle of light on the ground below. Gusts of wind buffeted the cozy house, and she squinted into the pelting rain to see who might be going out. Then the hinges creaked again and the light disappeared, plunging the outdoors into darkness once more.

Through the driving rain, a hint of movement drew her attention to a shadowy figure crossing the yard. Echo strained her eyes, but she could not make it out. Then, a flash of lightning, another, and another, lit the sky in quick succession. Echo caught her breath. Walking through the storm, hair long and flowing unbound around her in the tempest, her skirts fluttering in the wind, Mamai walked heedlessly into the rain toward the tip of the peninsula. Echo stared out the window, willing another lightning bolt to scatter the darkness. When it came, she saw her mother descending the rocky stairs that led to the beach. Her head soon disappeared below the cliffside, out of Echo's view.

Her head spun as she leaned her elbows on the windowsill. Where had Mamai gone? Why could she possibly need to be out in such a storm? No houses lay that way, so it couldn't be a sick neighbor. The docks were on the other side of the peninsula, and anyway, if there were a problem there, it would have been her father who attended to it. The mystery of it lay heavy on her thoughts as she awaited her mother's return.

But she did not return.

Echo's eyelids grew heavy. She struggled to keep them open, propping herself up in an uncomfortable position in an attempt to stay awake, but eventually she succumbed to the insistent embrace of sleep.

The crackling of pork sausages and the smell of frying mushrooms gently called Echo out of slumber. A glance out the window showed that the day had dawned gray and drizzly. She had slumped over in the night, her face pressed against the cold floorboards. Her neck had a fierce kink in it that she kneaded with her fingers as she hastily pulled on her dress and descended the ladder. Mamai stood over the stove, her hair bound up in its customary braid around her head, her cheeks red as she bent over the hot stove, a dusting of flour on her nose. She looked up and grinned at Echo.

"Good morning," she greeted her. "Could you run out to the barn and milk Grainne?"

Echo nodded a little blearily, her head still foggy with

sleep. There had been something she wanted to ask, something wild and fearsome from the night before, but she could not remember just now. Perhaps it had just been a dream. That must have been it. A dream. A strange dream, to be sure. Her brow furrowed as she strained to capture it and a flash of memory pierced the morning fog. Surely she had not actually seen her mother running out into the storm like a wild creature... Her glance suddenly registered the dress draped over the stove, her mother's dress, still damp and steaming as it dried.

"What happened to your dress?" Echo asked.

Mamai gave it an airy glance and smiled, her face filled with merry delight. "I got caught in the rain fetching eggs from the henhouse this morning," she explained. "It should have been you, you know. What were you doing, sleeping on the floor like that? I tried to wake you, but you seemed to need the extra rest this morning."

Echo shook her head. "I'm sorry. I didn't mean to sleep in. I'll go milk Grainne. Is Dadai down at the docks already?"

"No, he went out to look over the garden; he wants to begin hoeing soon. Though goodness knows after last night's storm it's too wet to be attempting that chore right now." Mamai gave a teasing grin. "You didn't sleep in that much; we haven't had breakfast."

Echo nodded and slipped outside. The rain had stopped and sunshine peeked out from behind the clouds, its warmth promising a lovely day. It wasn't until she was halfway to the barn that Echo realized the dress drying on the stove had been the same one her mother had worn the day before.

Grainne greeted her with a gentle lowing, and Echo patted her wide, soft nose as she entered the stall with stool and pail.

"Why would Mamai lie about how her dress got wet, Grainne?" she asked, streams of milk plinking into the empty bucket. "Or did I just dream it all? But then, I know I got out of bed because I fell asleep by my window. I woke up… eh, sore." She rolled her neck around, wincing as she stretched the tight muscles. She shook her head carefully. "Mamai and Dadai were acting strangely last night. I've seen it before, but I never really gave it much thought; does that make sense?"

The cow chewed a mouthful of hay with a sleepy look of unconcern, one ear flicking back as though twitching away a fly.

Echo sighed. "Maybe a neighbor took ill. But then, Mamai would have told me." She shrugged, hunching her shoulders up around her ears, the first, high pings giving way to the thick slosh of milk filling the bucket. "I'm making too much out of this, right? Right. That's all. I'm making it all up and there's nothing to worry about. The storm unsettled me and made me imagine things."

Her mind made up, she nodded firmly, pressing her lips together as she finished the milking. She covered the pail with a cloth to protect it from the light mist outside, then, with full pail swinging from her hand, she ducked back across the yard and into the house where she quickly plunked it on the table, her gaze deliberately avoiding the inexplicable dress hanging on the stove. She brushed the droplets out of her hair and poured the family's morning milk before tipping the remainder into the waiting pancheons where the cream would rise for the butter churning.

Mamai set out the plates heaped high with eggs and fried mushrooms, pork sausages, mealy pudding, and soft bread left over from the night before. Dadai came in, slipping out of his muddy boots and shaking a fine, glittering spray of water from his dark hair.

When they were all seated, Dadai read a passage from his worn Bible and they bowed together for their customary prayer of thanks. Her parents seemed their usual selves, talking of small household matters as they served themselves. But even though breakfast was usually Echo's favorite meal of the day, her appetite was lost in thought. Disobedient to her resolution in the barn, her mind flew from the table into the storm of the night before. Instead of diving into her meal as she usually did, she picked at her food, arranging and rearranging it on her plate, and sneaking glances at her parents across the table.

Where were you last night? Why did you lie to me this morning? She wanted to blurt out the questions.

"Are you not feeling well, sweetheart?" Mamai asked, her voice full of gentle concern.

Echo shook her head guiltily. "I'm just... not very hungry." She forced a smile and took a bite of eggs, chewing them with some effort. They tasted like ashes on her tongue.

"Did you not sleep well?" Dadai asked.

"I had weird dreams." Echo shrugged and trailed her fork around her plate some more.

"I found her sleeping on the floor this morning," Mamai said. "Echo, why weren't you in your bed?"

Echo wanted to ask Mamai the same thing. Heat rushed to her face as accusing questions sprang into her thoughts, but she clamped her lips tightly shut on the words bubbling up within her. If Mamai didn't want her to know why she was outside running toward the cliffs in a storm, she wasn't going to ask.

"I don't know," Echo mumbled, a surge of rebelliousness

making her feel irritable. She wished they would just leave her alone.

She could feel her parents sharing a concerned glance across the table and more guilt bloomed in her chest, but she stuffed it down, glaring at her bread. An uncomfortable silence filled the little cottage.

"Well." Dadai pushed his chair back. "I wish you would talk to us about whatever is bothering you, wood-sprite, but if you need time, I understand. With the rain today, the fishing will be good, which means the docks will be busier than usual, and I need to get to work. I'm late already."

He rose and rounded the table, kissing the top of Echo's head. He kissed Mamai, slipped into his boots, donned his oiled jacket and hat, and left, the door swinging shut behind him.

Mamai fixed Echo with a long stare. Then she gave a perplexed smile. "If you're done, you can wash up."

Echo rose and grabbed her apron off the hook before taking the bucket out to the pump to fill it, mentally chastising herself for forgetting to do this before breakfast so that the water would have already been heated through. Mamai's strange behavior was ruining more than just her sleep, she thought miserably. And really, if Mamai did not wish to tell her, then perhaps it simply wasn't any of Echo's business. Her parents did not keep secrets, she reasoned with herself. Perhaps Mamai had not gone anywhere; perhaps she had merely experienced a wild wish to walk along the edge of the seashore in the rain and look out at the furious waves. She loved the ocean, after all. Echo felt a twinge of remorse for the sullen way she had acted at the breakfast table.

A quiet sound behind her made her spin around. A waiflike figure greeted her and Echo stared for a moment before a name surfaced.

"Branna! What are you doing up here?" Echo grimaced at the unfriendly words that escaped her mouth. In all, puzzles and surprises seemed to be getting the better of her. "I mean... um..." she stammered, trying to think of a way to smooth out her rough greeting. "I didn't expect to see you... here... today." That wasn't any better. She cringed again and wished she could just melt into the ground. A memory of children dancing around her, their voices raised in jeering laughter, made her scowl.

Branna dug a bare toe into the sand, her eyes fixed downward. She gave a little shrug. "Just wondered if you might be interested in... in a picnic this afternoon."

Echo automatically opened her mouth to give an excuse, then stopped, considering. Perhaps it was time to lay her bitterness to rest. Branna's welcoming wave at the seaside the day before surfaced in Echo's mind and she wondered if it might be possible to rekindle a friendship. It might be nice, having a friend again. And Branna was always surrounded by other girls, drawing them to her like moths to a flame, while Echo... well, rudely asked visitors what they were doing at her house. Her cheeks warmed. In Branna's circle, she might finally find acceptance among the other children, or at least a cessation of mutters about the fae.

Besides, Echo had the feeling that, after last night, she might jump out of her skin if she stayed near the house. She gave a tentative nod.

"That sounds... nice."

Branna glanced up from the divots she was drawing with her toes, her blue eyes shining. "Really?"

"Yes," Echo said, this time with more conviction. "I have chores to do this morning, though."

"Of course!" A grin spread across Branna's face. "I thought maybe off in Glenthail's Meadow? This afternoon, when everything's had some time to dry off?"

"Oh, I love it there!" Echo enthused, then paused, trying to rein in her feelings before she started waxing poetic about the location, which would probably only scare Branna away. She searched her brain for a more appropriate response. "I'll... I'll bring scones."

Branna brightened. "Your mother's scones?"

Echo nodded. "Is anyone else coming?" she blurted, pleased with herself for having had the foresight to ask. It would have been embarrassing to find that she hadn't brought enough pastries to share.

Branna faltered. "I... no." She stared at the ground some more.

Echo frowned. It dawned on her that Branna was behaving strangely. This was the girl who never had trouble speaking to anyone. Even though Echo was no longer part of her inner circle, Branna's boisterous enthusiasm for conversation was not easy to miss. "Branna? Is everything all right?"

Branna's face reddened. "I just, um... you spend time in the Faeorn, right? I mean, not just the outskirts?"

Echo nodded, completely bewildered.

"I... I..." Branna's voice dropped to a whisper. "I saw something. I have to tell someone or I'll burst! But... I don't think anyone but you will believe me," she finished in a rush. "Meet me in the meadow!" she said, then dashed away, leaving Echo staring after her.

Was it all just a cruel joke? What could Branna have seen

that she didn't think people would believe? Or was Branna sincere?

Her stomach clenched. Echo of the Fae rang discordantly through her mind. She did not know if she could bear it if Branna joined her voice to the remembered ones.

She sighed, carrying the full bucket inside and setting it over the fire. She should have known that amicable overtures would have a catch. Why were people so exhausting and complicated? She could stay home, pretend the invitation never happened. But what if she were wrong? There was only one way to find out what Branna's true intentions were. She'd just have to be braced for a trick.

4

A PICNIC IN THE MEADOW

When her chores were finished, Echo informed her mother of her afternoon plans. Mamai smiled warmly and insisted she take a basketful of scones, even though Echo protested that she and Branna couldn't possibly eat that many by themselves.

Glenthail's Meadow lay nestled between two rocky cliffs near the western edge of the Faeorn. The hideaway boasted a pleasant, grassy area filled with wildflowers. A clear pond stood at the entrance, and sometimes shepherds would lead their sheep or goats to water there, but the adults found little other use for it. The village children, however, occasionally came for picnics or swimming or simply to gather from the valley's plentiful wildflowers.

Branna was waiting when Echo arrived, a large cloth spread out on the ground. She smiled brightly and jumped to her feet as Echo approached.

"You came!"

"I said I would," Echo replied with a shrug.

"Yes, but..." The younger girl trailed off, grimacing. Then she brightened. "Your mother's scones! What kind?"

"Ruseberry." Echo's face warmed as her words got tangled together. "Er, I mean... raspberry-rhubarb."

"Ooh!" Branna's eyes lit up and they sat down on a cloth laid out with large wedges of cheese, a pile of gooseberries, and bannocks with a sparkling jar of currant jam.

They dug into their picnic with the will of young farm-girls who have spent the morning working hard. Though once her plate was full, Echo picked at her food self-consciously, taking tiny bites and doing her best not to drop crumbs or jam all over herself.

"I'm so glad spring has finally arrived," Branna said. "It's so dreary in winter, and there are no picnics."

Echo nodded in agreement, but her mouth was full, so she made no attempt to reply.

After a little while of companionable munching, Branna spoke again. "How is your mother?"

A fleeting vision of wild wind and flashing lightning filled Echo's mind. "She is well," she replied carefully.

"I heard she helped deliver the O'Brien baby last week. Have you seen him yet?"

Echo nodded, warming to the conversation. "He's so tiny!" she confided. "But Mamai says his lungs are healthy." She chuckled, remembering how the baby had vocally proclaimed his hunger toward the end of their short visit.

"We are going to visit them tomorrow. I can't wait to see him." She flopped back on the blanket with a sigh. "I like to come here," Branna said, closing her eyes. "It's so peaceful. Like there's room to think without everyone crowding around pushing your thoughts out of the way. It's funny, but

I always feel less lonely out here by myself than anywhere else."

Echo studied the other girl, carefully hiding her surprise. Branna, lonely? Could someone always surrounded by friends feel lonely? She wasn't sure. But then, Echo herself almost never felt lonely, and she had certainly never had a crowd flocking around her the way Branna always did. What might it be like, she wondered, to be surrounded by people and not feel genuine comfort with any of them?

The silence stretched out between them and Echo realized with an uncomfortable twinge that she should probably say something. Should she respond to Branna's comment about the meadow, or ask if she really felt lonely? Or had too much time passed for her to reply to that statement? She fidgeted with a fold of her skirt, plucking crumbs off it and flicking them into the grass. It was her turn to say something —of that, she was certain.

"So... you..." Echo bit the inside of her cheek. "You said you saw something strange in the forest?"

Branna sat up, her face alight with excitement. "Not in the forest, exactly. More... well... maybe under it."

"Um... under it?" Echo winced. Nothing like living up to her name.

Branna leaned forward, a strange expression flooding into her eyes as she lowered her voice. "You know the Guardians?"

Echo nodded. The two massive, ancient oak trees stood between the forest and the village, towering over the little school yard. They had grown up so close together that their bases had become conjoined, and their combined girth was easily fourteen meters. Everyone called them the Guardians because they looked like soldiers standing at attention, and because they marked the boundary of the Faeorn. Playing around their base was the closest most of the children would get to the ancient greenwood. The most notable thing about them, however, was the large hollowed-out area at the base of one of the trunks. The space inside was large enough for several children to fit inside comfortably, and it had been a favorite spot for imaginative play when they were young. Many young boys had become pirates in that hideout, while the girls tended to play house and have tea parties with their dolls. Echo had rarely been inside the hollow, never feeling assertive enough to claim her turn.

"Well," Branna continued, her voice dropping to a conspiratorial whisper, "I was tending the goats and not really paying attention when I suddenly realized they'd grazed down into the school yard. I didn't want them to muddy up our play yard, so I shooed them out, but they scattered into the Faeorn, so I had to go dashing about, chasing them all away from the trees before they went too far." She shuddered.

Echo nodded again, hanging on every word and glad that Branna did not seem to need encouragement to continue talking.

"When I had them all gathered back up, I was hot and tired. The goats were behaving themselves, so I thought I'd go explore a bit in the little hollow, you know, since nobody else was around."

Echo smiled a little. She had often wished for a chance to have the Guardians all to herself, but she didn't usually go that way when she wandered in the forest, as it was too near the village. While she didn't care much what others thought of her, there was no reason to go handing them gossip, and there would certainly be muttering in the village if they knew that the "strange McIntyre lass" was exploring the haunted forest.

"But I couldn't find the opening!" Branna announced.

"What?" Echo asked, wondering if she had missed some key piece of the other girl's story.

Branna fixed her with a serious stare. "The hollow, it wasn't there. It was getting dark, so I thought maybe I'd missed it. I walked all the way around the trees three times trying to remember where it was." She gave Echo a knowing look and fell silent.

Echo stared back for a long moment before she realized that Branna was waiting for her to speak. "Oh!" she said, racking her brain for something more intelligent. "Did... did you ever find it?"

"I did!" Branna frowned. "I don't know how I missed it the first two times, but then on my third time around... I saw it, right where it was supposed to be. But..." She hesitated, tugging on a lock of her dark hair. "Well, then I noticed a weird blue light glowing inside. I couldn't see it very well, just a tiny flicker, but it was there. I saw it as plain as I can see you."

"Did you go inside? Could you see what was making the light?" Now that Echo was caught up in the tale, the question leapt out easily.

Branna shook her head vigorously. "No! It... it frightened me. I kind of gave a shout and herded the flock home as fast as I could."

"So..." The thrall of excitement ended as abruptly as the story, and Echo's skepticism returned. "Then what do you think it was?"

Branna shrugged, looking suddenly uncomfortable.

But Echo's curiosity had the better of her now. "Maybe

one of the boys left a lantern inside and you couldn't see it until it got darker?"

"I don't think so," Branna said. "Besides, the light was decidedly blue. I've never seen a lantern glow blue."

"If the glass was blue..." Echo mused. "Do you think it might have been a prank of some kind? Somebody trying to scare you?"

Branna bit her lip. "I don't think it was a prank. Besides, nobody knew I would be there. I was just following my goats."

"Then what?"

"I think... I think it was a... fae light," Branna whispered.

The bottom dropped out of Echo's world as the betrayal sliced through her. So this had all been a prank, after all. A chance to laugh at the awkward girl who spent her days in the haunted forest. Echo of the Fae. Firmly clutching her dignity, she stood, brushed the crumbs from her skirt, and slung her mother's basket over her arm.

"Thank you for inviting me; the picnic was lovely," she said stiffly. "But I have to get home now."

"Echo!" Branna jumped to her feet, reaching out to clutch at her arm.

Echo pulled away from the other girl. She gave a forced, mirthless laugh as tears began to blur her vision. "I'll bet you all thought you were so... so... clever, coming up with that story."

"No!" Branna looked close to tears. "Echo, it isn't like that!"

"Well, you can keep your bannocks and your silly ghost stories and your horrival teasing. I prefer the forest and... and... anything to all of you!" With that slightly garbled pronouncement, Echo turned and fled blindly from the meadow. She didn't want to wait for the other girls to come out from wherever they were hiding to laugh at her. Hot tears coursed down her cheeks as she ran. She ought to have known better than to seek friendship from Branna. Her place was on the fringes of their company, not in the center; she knew that, and everyone else knew it, too.

When she reached home she paused at the doorway, wiping her face on her sleeve. Wherever Mamai had been the night before suddenly did not matter as much as it had that morning. All she wanted was to curl up in her mother's arms and let her soothe away the sting of Branna's teasing.

5

UNEXPLAINED SORROWS

a fter the humiliation at the picnic, Echo stayed close to home. Her days fell into a steady rhythm of chores and helping her parents with the spring planting. The days grew ever warmer: buds began to form on the trees and the first garden sprouts poked up through the dark soil.

However, as spring progressed, Echo couldn't help but notice certain oddities around home she had never been aware of before. Little things that meant nothing on their own began to add up into an invisible, yet undeniable presence. Looks shared between her parents she did not understand, snatches of late-night conversation when they thought she was asleep, and a strange sorrow in her mother's eyes that Echo could not comprehend.

A week passed, and then another. The last of the spring chill dwindled and gave way to the full force of summer, which brought a slew of furious storms.

Echo spent more than one night by her window, watching her mother's figure inexplicably disappear into the wind and rain, but she always fell asleep long before her return. In the daylight, when her parents smiled and went about their daily routines without a word or whisper of the strange behavior, Echo wondered if she had dreamed it all, but then would catch another covert, knowing look passing between them, and the questions would revive, breeding impalpable dread that surrounded her with a thick, suffocating fog. Echo grew tense and jumpy and found herself racing through her chores and escaping more and more often into the forest. She told herself it was because she had permission, but in reality she knew she was running away. However, there was no escaping her fears—she carried those with her.

One early morning, Echo came down to find her mother sitting in her rocking chair, her head bowed, her long hair down about her shoulders like a curtain of sunlight. Echo frowned. The sky outside held only the faintest glow emanating from beneath the horizon, but this behavior was abnormal. Mamai did not usually sit idly once awake. She crept over to her mother's side and laid a hand on her shoulder.

"Mamai?" she ventured.

Runa looked up with a start. "Oh, Echo. Forgive me, sweetheart, I must have dozed off over my knitting this morning. I'll get breakfast on straight-away." But she did not rise from the chair; instead she seemed to fade into the distance again, staring at her hands.

Echo frowned. The knitting basket sat untouched on the other side of the room, but before she could mention this, she caught a glimpse of her mother's eyes. They were red-rimmed as though she had been weeping.

"Mamai? Are you ill?"

"What?" Mamai asked, her tone distracted. "No."

"Is someone ill?" A sudden fear fluttered in her heart. "Is Dadai well?"

Dadai chose that moment to come through the door. "Is Dadai what?" he asked with a grin, his demeanor clearly one of good health.

"Mamai hasn't started breakfast yet," Echo informed him, her tone quiet and bewildered.

Her parents' eyes met across the small cottage and Dadai nodded slowly. "I can see that. Well, perhaps we could just have some bread and cheese this morning."

Mamai smiled softly and Dadai knelt by the rocking chair, wrapping his arms around his wife. Runa gave a deep sigh and leaned her cheek on the top of his head, her eyes squeezed tightly shut. For a long moment, they sat there. Echo stared, wondering what it all meant. She felt awkward and out of place, but she couldn't look away, either.

Then Dadai rose, kissed his wife's forehead gently, and told her to go back to bed. She nodded and drifted away into their room. Echo watched her go, a terrible and frightening emptiness opening in her chest. Dadai did not seem to notice, but merely stepped into the kitchen and began cutting thick slices of bread.

"Echo, why don't you go get a block of cheese from the spring house?"

"What's wrong with Mamai?" she asked.

"Mamai will be fine. Please go get the cheese."

"But..."

"Echo!" He did not raise his voice, but the sharp command told her that this was not the moment to argue. She fled to the spring house where she stood for a long moment, trying to calm the ominous thudding of blood in her ears. When she had managed to regain some modicum of composure, she returned with the cheese.

Her father carved several large chunks off the block and then brought the plates to the table. Echo sat with him, picking at her bread. It was strange, not having their customary sausage or eggs or mealy pudding. It was strange, not having Mamai there, her gentle smile filling the entire cottage.

"Is Mamai ill?"

"No." Dadai's tone was gentler now. He heaved a sigh. "This time of year always brings some difficult memories for your mother."

"It does?" Echo wondered why she had never noticed this before.

Her father nodded. "It's nothing you have to worry about, though. She just needs a day of rest. She will be back to her normal self by tomorrow. You know, perhaps a day of rest might be good for everyone. Why don't you pack yourself a picnic and go visit the Faeorn? You can take one of my books with you, if you like."

She was too startled by this offer to even be excited at the prospect. "What about my chores?"

"I'll do them for you before I head down to the docks."

A grin started to pull at the corners of her mouth, but then she paused. "No, I'll do my own chores. You don't get a day of rest, and if you do my work, then you're doing more than usual. That's not fair."

Dadai's eyes warmed with pride and he reached his arm across the table to tug lightly on her dark braid. "My tender-hearted wood-sprite." He rested his chin on his hands and gazed at her contemplatively. "How about this: I'll let you help me with the chores if you promise to tell me about some of your friends in the Faeorn. I hear there's a squirrel with a liking for honey-cakes."

That brought a faint smile to her face. "Deal."

Working on the dishes together, Echo chattered eagerly about the animals who had come to trust her and how they would eat out of her hand and listen to her stories. Dadai was fascinated by all of them.

"You don't go too deep into the forest, do you?" he interjected at one point.

Echo shook her head. "No," she assured him. "But farther than the outer rim. That's not really the Faeorn, you know."

"I know." A shadow crossed his face, but then he shook it away.

"Have you been inside the Faeorn?" Echo was suddenly curious. Her father had told her countless stories about his adventures at sea, but she had never heard him talk about any exploits on land. She had always assumed that he'd spent his time ashore more or less inert, but now she realized that seemed uncharacteristic of her intrepid father.

"Once."

"Just once?" Echo queried.

Her father's motions slowed as he rubbed the last plate with a towel before placing it in the well-organized cupboard he had built for his wife. Then he jerked his head toward the yard. "Let's go muck out Grainne's stall."

She trotted along behind him, her questions pressing against her insides, but Dadai hadn't dismissed the topic, so she kept her lips pressed tightly together and waited while they gathered the muck fork and wheelbarrow.

Echo led the docile dairy cow out into the back pasture where she could graze, then took a few thick flakes of straw from the bale and joined her father in the stall.

"I've been inside the Faeorn a number of times, of course," Dadai said, tossing soiled straw into the wheelbarrow. "But only once did I venture into the depths of the forest."

"When?"

Dadai threw another forkful of straw and then lowered the pitchfork to the ground and rested his chin on the top of the long handle. Echo started as she caught his gaze, for in it was a hint of the same sorrow she had seen in Mamai's eyes that morning.

"A long time ago."

"Dadai? Does this story have something to do with why Mamai is so sad?"

His eyebrows rose and he pulled off one of his leather work gloves to rub his face. "Why do you ask that?"

Echo shrugged, suddenly uncomfortable. "Just a guess," she mumbled.

Echo waited, but her father did not continue his story. While he took the muck out to the manure pile, she pulled apart the flakes she'd brought and carpeted the stall in fresh straw. By the time she'd finished, her father had put away the tools.

When they had finished, Dadai wrapped an arm around his daughter's shoulders and pulled her close. "You guessed right," he said in a low tone. "But you see, that particular story is not mine to tell—not mine alone, anyway. Someday, Mamai and I will tell you the tale. But not today. Today, you enjoy exploring the Faeorn and reading whichever book you like. Today, you go have your own adventures."

Echo nodded, disappointment mingling with the excitement of a day to herself.

Her father squeezed her shoulders once more then smiled down at her. "Be back in time for dinner."

Together, they made quick work of the rest of Echo's chores. With a book safely tucked in a shoulder bag, she made her way once again into the cool depths of the Faeorn, shedding her worry like a sweater on a warm spring day. She tossed some seeds about and produced a honey cake, waiting for her animal friends to join her. When they did, however, they ignored her offerings, their movements agitated. Her squirrel friend raced up and down the trunk of a nearby tree, chittering frantically. The little birds hopped among the pine needles, oblivious to the handfuls of seeds and nuts she had scattered. The bunny nosed its way through the snowdrops, but dashed away when she looked at it, only to creep back a moment later.

Echo wished she could understand their speech. "What is it?" she asked, knowing she would get no answer. "What has you all so worked up this morning?"

Her mouth opened in shock as they all sat straight up and looked at her, every feather, tail, and nose perfectly still. Then they turned as one and started hopping or fluttering away, all headed in the same direction. When Echo looked that way, the animals and birds grew excited, scampering and flying in circles at the edge of her clearing.

"What's over there?" she muttered. She clambered over a fallen tree and around underbrush too dense for her to push through. Her friends followed at a safe distance, their chirps and chattering coaxing her onward. Here, the forest grew thicker and deeper. A new sound reached her ears: the sound of running water. A moment later, she burst through the trees and found herself on the bank of a lovely little creek. A fluttering sound filled the air and she looked up to find herself staring straight into the angry, open beak of a massive owl.

Echo yelped and shrank back, throwing her arms up protectively over her head. But nothing happened. She risked a glance and realized that the owl was trapped. It had flown into a tangle of vines and become enmeshed in the ivy. Even now it hung upside down, its entire body drooping with weariness.

"You poor thing," Echo whispered. "How long have you been stuck there?"

The owl struggled, beating its wings, but the effort was futile and held a measure of defeat.

"Since last night, I'd guess." Echo walked around beneath the owl, studying the creature and the situation. "I've never seen one like you before," she crooned soothingly.

The white, heart-shaped face was familiar; it looked like the owls that roosted in the rafters of their barn. But where their pinions were a soft brown, this one was clad only in feathers of the purest white. Hearing her voice, it craned its head about, staring down at her with dark, knowing eyes. Along the left wing she noticed that it was not completely white, after all, but bore a golden chevron picked out in the feathers near its shoulder.

"I'm going to get you out," Echo said. She had spotted a way up, and from there, it would be easy to use her little garden knife to cut the ivy and loose the owl. "But you have to promise not to attack me while I'm climbing up there," she continued.

Reaching up, she grasped hold of two branches sticking out of the trunk at right angles. Scrabbling with her feet, she pulled herself up until she settled on the lowest limbs. Now that she had gotten past the first hurdle, Echo quickly climbed a few more branches until she reached the one she wanted. Wrapping her arms and legs around the branch, she scooted out over the tangle of vines. She had positioned herself well, but she worried that the bird might simply plummet once she had sawn through the ivy.

Carefully, so as not to lose her balance, she pulled her knife out of her satchel. At the glint of metal, the owl let out a frantic hoot and flapped its wings erratically, its chest heaving.

"Shhhh, shhhh!" Echo raised her free hand, gripping the branch with her knees for balance. "This little thing couldn't hurt you even if I meant to. It's just to help me get those vines untangled."

The owl cocked its head, swaying slightly, its body calming. Echo selected a vine and began to cut at it. The owl watched her unblinkingly. Below her, the sun sparkled brightly on the rippling waters of the creek. The ivy was thicker than it looked. Perspiration beaded on her forehead and dripped down into her eyes as she tediously sheared off first one vine, then another. The blade was meant more for pruning tomato plants and beheading spent blooms, not for sawing through the tough, woody ivy. But eventually, she sawed through the last strand and the entire net broke apart. The owl dropped, and Echo held her breath in concern, but then it twisted in the air and spread its wings to glide out over the creek. It fluttered to the ground on the other side of the water and stared for a long moment at the strange girl up in the tree.

Then, in a rush of silent wings, it rose into the air and flew away, up the stream and into the upper reaches of the Faeorn.

"Goodbye," Echo called after it. "I hope your family hasn't been worried."

When it had disappeared into the spring-green canopy,

she carefully made her way back to the tree trunk and worked her way down to the forest floor. She went immediately to the creek and plunged her hot, sweaty face into its cool waters, drinking deeply of the sparkling liquid as she came up. Then, heedless and thrilled by the shock of glittering cold, she waded into the stream, reveling in the coolness on her bare feet and around her ankles that shivered up her entire body. She laughed and danced in the brook, staring off to where it vanished into the depths of the forest and wondering where it would take her if she followed it. The position of the sun, still in the eastern half of the sky, told her that the entire rescue had taken no more than twenty minutes. The day of freedom stretched out before her and a desire for adventure swelled in her breast. Hefting her satchel higher on her shoulder, Echo's feet made little splashes in the water as she followed its glistening path deeper into the Faeorn.

Little water bugs scattered before her steps as Echo splashed along, following the stream. At first, the water barely covered her ankles, but it grew deeper until she could no longer hold her skirt up high enough to avoid soaking the hem. She scrambled up onto the bank and clambered over the large rocks that bordered the waterway. She navigated her way along in this way until the banks receded and the water grew shallow once again. Sunlight dappled the water and little minnows darted about her toes as she resumed her wading.

The rustle of leaves and glimpses through the trees told her that her furry and feathered companions remained nearby, though they often darted off on side-quests of their own.

When she tired of walking, she climbed up out of the

creek and found a comfortable spot to rest. She pulled out Dadai's worn copy of The Odyssey and spent a pleasant afternoon reading.

She returned home when the daylight began to fade. A peek through her parents' open door showed her that Mamai was still in her room, curled up on the large bed.

"Mamai? Can I get you anything?" Echo whispered.

There was no answer, so she tiptoed into the bedroom. Mamai's eyes were closed, her face drawn and full of grief, even in her sleep. A prickle of worry pierced Echo's heart, but she crept quietly out of the room and began making supper for herself and her father.

When Dadai came home he stepped through the door quietly, without his usual boisterous entrance. He smiled appreciatively at the food Echo had prepared and sat down to eat with her.

"Is Mamai sleeping?" he asked.

Echo nodded.

"Good. We'll let her sleep. Tomorrow will be better."

"I don't understand," Echo said, fear welling within her. "What's wrong with Mamai? I thought you said she was just sad."

"Grief is a funny thing," Dadai replied after a long silence. "Sometimes you can even forget all about it. But then sometimes, it just kind of overwhelms you, pulls you down into it and holds you prisoner."

"I wish there was something I could do."

"Just be yourself, wood-sprite." Dadai winked at her. "And give Mamai lots of extra hugs."

6

THE DISCOVERY

*J*ust as Dadai had predicted, the next day Mamai seemed back to her usual self. But Echo could not shake the shadow that had fallen over her own heart. She stayed close to the house for the next several weeks as spring progressed with its usual alacrity.

The days grew steadily warmer and suddenly buds sprouted on the trees and then burst into tiny new leaves. Flowers began to bloom in the meadows and sprouts pushed up through the soil of their garden, peeking out at the world above.

The spring storms waned, and with them, her mother's strange behavior. May gave way to June, and Echo's worries from the turbulent springtime waned and grew dim. She found herself missing the Faeorn, and losing herself in daydreams.

One morning, after Echo had absentmindedly dropped one plate and two glasses while washing dishes after breakfast, Mamai pressed her lips together and firmly shooed her out of the house.

"You've been as broody as Grainne on a wet day," she remonstrated. "Go on. Get outside and away from the house. I have some neighbors to check on this afternoon, and I can't keep cleaning up after you or I'll never get down to the village before sunset."

"Thank you, Mamai!" Echo grabbed up her satchel and raced out through the door, bare feet pounding on the grass. Behind her, the door slammed against its frame and she could hear her mother's exasperated voice calling after her, but she didn't stop. She pelted toward the Faeorn like a wild thing freed from a cage.

Once inside the trees, she slowed, drinking in the peaceful quiet of the mighty oaks. The jumpy, restless feeling that had been irritating her for days calmed as she took deep draughts of the forest air.

Aimlessly, she wandered deeper into the forest until she came to the stream. She stepped down to its edge and scooped up a handful of water to drink, then patted her cool, wet hands to her face, warm from her run across the fields. The creek was gentle and shallow here, wending its way south toward the village and north, deeper into the forest. Echo knelt on the bank, eyeing the strip of water. She had promised not to go too deeply into the forest, but something called to her, like a physical string pulling her, and an impetuous curiosity to see what lay at the heart of the forest.

After two hours of hiking, the winding path of the stream ended in a burbling waterfall and the remains of an ancient stone bridge that had long since collapsed. It was covered in a soft green moss, and its fallen stones had created a small but ambitious rapid in the midst of the chattering creek.

Enchanted by the picturesque, fairy tale setting she had discovered, Echo's desire to continue any further faded. With nimble movements, she clambered up the ancient, crumbling steps and looked down. In days long past, her little creek must have once been a far mightier beast, she thought, to warrant such a bridge. The stones shimmered in the sunlight with flecks of gold and a sense of awe froze her in her tracks. A stillness filled the wood, and she could easily imagine that in ancient days this had once been a place of importance. A power still thrummed in the stones, a sleeping power, perhaps, but not diminished beyond recognition. A cloud passed over the sun and the feeling broke. Echo shook herself out of the fancy and carefully settled herself down on the broken edge of the bridge, letting her feet dangle, attuning to the sounds of the forest and the cheerful music of the running water below. Turning out her pockets, she revealed a meager handful of crumbs and seeds and scattered them about, then she leaned back against what was left of the stone railing and took the book out of her little satchel.

She quickly fell into the story; it was one of her favorites, and she whiled away the hours entranced by the words that never failed to spirit her away into another world. It was not until she found herself squinting to make out the text that she finally looked up. She rose swiftly, her heart thudding in her chest in sudden fright. The shadows around her had grown long and ominous. The woodland creatures had long since departed, having finished the last of her gifts. Through openings in the canopy she caught glimpses of large, angry storm clouds beginning to roll across the darkening sky, and through the trees she could just make out a faint line of gold stretching along the far horizon, signaling the approach of night.

She leapt down the moss-carpeted slant of the bridge, tucking her father's book back into the bag slung over her shoulder as she went. Her bare feet slapped the ground as she raced along the bank of the creek, following it back to the spot where she had entered the forest. The daylight continued to wane and twilight had caught her before she reached the edge of the Faeorn. A gust of wind whipped at her skirt. The rumble of the hooves of heavenly horses galloping across the sky reverberated through her chest. In the dusky, silver light, Echo thought she saw shapes moving in the trees—specters with ghostly, outstretched hands; malevolent eyes concealed in the brush; long-limbed, clawed things ready to pounce when her back was turned. She whirled about, but all she saw were trees, their branches waving in the restless breeze that heralded the coming storm. She chided herself for letting her imagination run amok, but she was still late getting home, so she felt perfectly justified in hastening her pace.

When the last fallen log had been scaled and she saw the grassy field stretching out before her, Echo broke into a sprint. Her hair streaked out behind her as she ran for home, her heart pounding a rhythm of trepidation she had never felt toward the Faeorn before.

She flew home and burst through the front door, a myriad of apologies already pouring from her lips, but they evaporated as soon as she entered the cottage.

The house was empty. No Mamai stood in the kitchen, one hand on her hip, lines of worry creasing her forehead. The stove stood cold and forlorn in the corner. The lantern on the table waited, unlit. No smells of baking bread emanated from the oven. No Dadai sat on the bench, taking off his boots, a teasing grin lighting his eyes. Just a stark, desolate silence.

Worried that her mother had fallen into one of her

sorrows again, Echo quietly checked her parents' room. The bedding was rumpled and unkempt as usual—Mamai could do many things, but tidiness often eluded her—but the chamber was empty.

Echo leaned against the doorframe, panting with exertion. A sense of abandonment welled within her. Where had Mamai gone? For a moment she toyed with the idea that her mother had gone out into the forest searching for her, but she quickly rejected that thought. Mamai had known where she intended to go, and it was not yet so late that she would have grown worried. For a wild moment, Echo thought of the sea and its hungry, grasping waves and a primal, irrational terror clawed its way up behind her eyes. But she shook this away with a snort of disgust. The sea was just the sea. Wherever Mamai had gone, there would be a good reason, and both she and Dadai would be home soon. And that meant there was only one thing to do.

Echo tramped outside to the pump and washed her face and hands, getting a long, cold drink while she was at it. Thunder rumbled again in the distance, but the clouds had yet to release the rain. Echo barely spared a glance for the dark storm front as she marched back inside and began gathering the things she would need for supper. Mamai was often called away to tend to the sick or injured in the village. She also had a comforting presence, the people of Ennis Rosliath all agreed, and so she would sometimes simply go and sit with those who were lonely or grieving. In fact, hadn't Mamai said something about going to the village this afternoon? Echo had not been listening carefully, but she thought she remembered hearing her mother say that. She nodded firmly to herself, trying to ignore the dull, insistent roar of the waves rolling against the cliffs far below the house.

Well, if Mamai had indeed gone into town, Echo's job was to have supper ready.

She stoked the fire and began chopping vegetables while the cottage filled with a pleasant warmth. She spotted a bowl on the counter covered with a cheesecloth and found that Mamai had left some dough to rise, which it had obediently done. Echo punched it down with perhaps unwarranted force and then separated it into segments which she worked into a braid, thinking how proud Mamai would be to see it. There was something calming about working with the dough, too, and a pleasure Echo always felt in creating something not only delicious, but beautiful. The work consumed her, and her dark thoughts fled as the wind kicked up outside, battering the snug house.

The bread, however, did not want to cooperate with her vision, and Echo soon grew frustrated with the dough. After several attempts, she gave up. Irritably, she pressed the ends together and shoved the uneven mess into the oven with an exasperated huff. It might not look pretty, but it would still taste good.

Next, Echo turned her attention to the rest of the meal. The root cellar held some potted meat ready for cooking, and one of Mamai's precious jars of blackberry preserves would go well with the bread and the new butter Echo had churned earlier that morning.

Shielding the lantern carefully against the gusts of wind, she walked the short distance to the cellar and pulled open the door to the wooden stairs. At the bottom, a cool, imperturbable darkness suffused the familiar shelves, and she breathed in the musty, earthy scent of the space. The preserves were stacked neatly on their own special shelf near the entrance, and she tucked a jar into a large pocket of her apron. Near the back, as she reached for another jar, something caught her attention. She squinted through the gloom, raising the lantern higher. Off to the right, in the back corner, it looked as though part of the wall had broken. With a frown, she left the jar on the shelf and went to investigate. Dadai had taught her to always be on the lookout for signs of wear anywhere on their small farm. It was better to catch a small problem early, he said, than to wait until it became a crisis.

However, when she reached the back of the cellar, she realized that the wall had not, in fact, broken. Instead, the lantern revealed a small, partially open door she had never seen before. A quick survey revealed that the shelves on the back wall had been built right over the door in an ingenious design that hid its seams perfectly. Had it not been open, she would have never seen it.

Curiosity flooded her veins with shivering dread and prickling delight. What could be behind a hidden door in a cellar, of all places? Perhaps the door hid a secret tunnel, or a treasure her father had discovered on one of his sea voyages as a youth! Eagerly, she opened it wider and ducked inside.

The room beyond was small, just big enough for her to crouch inside. The roof sloped abruptly, tapering to the ground. Clearly, this alcove had been dug after the rest of the cellar. There was a pang of disappointment that she had not uncovered a secret passageway, but the disappointment fled as soon as she noticed the chest.

Constructed of rough-hewn wood, it was the sole occupant of the secret room. No jewels encrusted its sides. No padlock forbade intrusion. In fact, the chest did not even have a latch that Echo could see. And yet, the mystery of it captivated her. It looked exactly like the ordinary sea-chests she had seen her father load onto ships down at the docks, the ones that sailors packed with their belongings whenever they shipped out on a longer voyage. Though his sailing days had long since ended, her father kept a trunk beneath the window in their cottage, where Mamai used it for storing blankets. But Echo had not realized he owned another. What could it contain? What treasure could her father possibly possess that he would hide it in a secret room concealed in their cellar?

Cautiously, she shuffled forward on her knees and placed a hand on the lid. But then she hesitated. Whatever lay inside had been hidden for a reason. Perhaps she should not disturb it. For the briefest eyeblink she contemplated retreating, closing the door behind her, and forgetting the room and the chest existed. But in the next heartbeat she had already lifted the lid.

7

THE SECRET OF THE CHEST

"*E*cho!" Mamai's voice echoed through the small cottage along with the wind that howled through the open door. Behind her, night had fallen, yet the rain had not.

Echo looked up dully from where she sat at the table, her plate clean and empty. Her mother closed the door against the wind and hung up her cloak, setting the basket on the floor.

"I am so sorry you came home to an empty house." Mamai sat down at the table with a weary sigh. "And it only just occurred to me that I didn't even leave a note. Matilda O'Caughrean went into labor four weeks early and she was having a hard time of it, so they sent little Daniel to come get me. It's been a long day." She rubbed the back of her hand wearily across her forehead. "That braided loaf looks beautiful." Her brow wrinkled. "Weren't you hungry?"

Echo glanced at the untouched bread sitting on the table, the thing she had been so proud of... had it even been an hour ago? She shook her head listlessly.

"I'll get you some dinner." The words were mechanical in tone as Echo rose to ladle out a serving of the meat and vegetable stew that she had cooked. She set the bowl in front of her mother, who looked up at her with misgiving written plainly in her eyes, but Echo couldn't hold her mother's gaze.

Just then, the sky finally let loose and raindrops fell in a low roar onto the roof above them. The door flew open once more and Gareth burst in. He shrugged out of his coat and sat down to remove his boots.

"I had to hightail it to beat the rain," he announced cheerfully. Then he paused. "What's wrong?"

"Matilda had her baby this evening," Runa said, rising to greet him. "I was with her all day."

Gareth peered down at her in concern. "Are they well?"

"Mother and baby are healthy and recovering splendidly."

"Good, good." Dadai looked relieved. He frowned. "Then why do I feel like I just interrupted a funeral?"

Mamai did not say anything, but they both turned to look at Echo, who shrugged uncomfortably under the force of their combined regard.

"I'm not feeling well," Echo mumbled. "I was thinking about going to bed early tonight."

Mamai came over and put a hand on Echo's forehead. "You feel a little warm." She turned to Gareth. "And she has no appetite; didn't eat a bite of supper."

"May I go to bed, Mamai?" Echo pleaded. She wanted to flee to her room, but she knew if she did her mother would follow her. "I think I'm just tired."

Her parents shared another glance. Then her mother nodded. "Yes, that's fine. I'll come check on you in a little while."

Echo nodded and climbed up the ladder where she changed into her nightgown and wilted onto her quilt. She clutched at the worn, familiar fabric, trying to find a semblance of comfort in the leafy patterns Mamai had sewn there for her years ago. She could hear the muffled voices of her parents below and she pulled her thin pillow over her head, trying to drown out any fragments of their conversation. She did not want to listen to them talking. Did not want to hear them worrying about her. If only she hadn't needed to go to the cellar. If only she hadn't noticed the secret door. If only she had left the chest closed. Why couldn't she have just left it alone?

But she had looked inside. And she could never take it back. She might not understand everything about what she had found, but she understood enough. Confused misery soaked the mattress beneath her face until she drifted off to sleep.

She startled awake, muddled and wondering what had roused her.

Why was the air so stifling? Her pillow had traveled over her head for some reason. She sat up, blinking in the darkness. No, she had fallen asleep like that. What had intruded on her sleep? The door?

The door!

Echo came fully awake as the events of the day crashed back over her. The sound of the door slamming shut made her cringe. She pulled her blanket up around her chin as she huddled in her bed, wondering what was happening downstairs in the middle of the night.

She heard a tinkling of glass and then the faint glow of a lantern gleamed between her floorboards.

"Gareth!"

Echo had never heard her mother sound so panicked. She frowned. Had someone brought bad news?

"Runa? What is it?" Dadai's voice sounded groggy, as if he, too, had been asleep.

"Gareth, it's gone! How could you? How could you?" Mamai was sobbing now, her voice rising to a hysterical shriek. "I always come back, I thought you trusted me. But it's gone. And worse, they're both gone!"

The sound of Dadai's feet thumping across the floor-boards. "What?" his voice sounded more alert. "What do you mean, they're gone? How could they be gone? How could you think I... no! Runa!"

Her mother's voice escalated into unintelligible wailing.

"Runa, you're going to wake Echo... Runa! I didn't take them! I swear to you. We will find them, I promise; please trust me as you always have."

Confusion jangled about in Echo's brain. It was as she had feared, everything was true. She knew they must be talking about the contents of the chest. But how did Mamai know where they were? Was that why the secret door had been open? Then... did she mean to leave them both? A furi-ous, vengeful part of her wanted to close her eyes and go back to sleep, pretend she hadn't heard. But her mother's mournful keening ripped her heart to shreds, and she knew she could not bear to be the cause of such pain.

Trembling, she crawled out of bed. Her heart pounding like a caged animal against her ribs, Echo descended her ladder. The floorboards were cold beneath her bare feet. She stared at her parents, and for a moment the entire world grew dark around the edges and she felt as though she might faint. But she took a deep breath and lifted a blanket in the corner, revealing the two seal skins she had found within the chest hidden in the cellar.

"Dadai didn't take them. I did!" she choked out. The last thing she remembered was the looks of horrified surprise on her parents' faces, and then she did faint, crumpling to the floor.

When she awoke, Echo found herself sitting in Mamai's chair. Her mother knelt at her side, holding a damp, cool cloth to her forehead, and Dadai stood over the stove heating water.

"She's awake." Mamai's voice sounded relieved.

Dadai turned and smiled at her. "How does a warm cup of tea sound?"

"Good," Echo croaked.

"I am so sorry," Mamai murmured, pushing aside a few damp strands of Echo's hair. "We should have told you long ago."

"Told me?" Echo asked. Then it all came crashing back and hot tears stung her eyes as bitter fury filled her chest. "Told me what? That my mother isn't human? Or that my father is keeping her captive?"

Her parents stared at each other across the cottage, and her father's mouth dropped open.

"Echo," Mamai said, her tone reproving.

"Is that what you think is going on here?" Dadai asked, sinking onto the kitchen bench with a heavy thud. He shook his head, his eyes a gaping wound bleeding sorrow. "No wonder you were so distraught," he murmured faintly.

"Well?" Echo demanded, glaring at them both. "Isn't that what happened? I know the stories as well as anyone else. You're a selkie, aren't you?" she demanded of her mother.

"Yes," Runa replied wearily.

"You spend part of your life as a human, and part of it as a seal, isn't that right?"

"Yes, darling." Mamai sighed.

"The stories say that selkies don't stay on land willingly. If that is true, then Dadai must have tricked you and stolen your skin, and that's why you can't leave, even though you want to, and why it was hidden away in the cellar," Echo burst out. She glared furiously at both of them and then buried her face in her arms as her world crashed down around her ears.

The tea kettle began to sing, but nobody tended to it.

"I think it's best if we tell her the whole story," Dadai said, his voice quiet.

Echo peeked up over her arms and watched her mother hasten to her husband's side, her arms encircling his shoulders. She kissed his cheek, her long hair falling forward.

"Yes, darling," Mamai replied. "The time has come. Perhaps we have already kept the secret for too long. But perhaps it is not too late to undo the damage."

Gareth looked over at Echo, and his wounded gaze pierced her to the core. He sighed and rose, lifting the insistent kettle and pouring the promised cup of tea. Mamai pulled two chairs over near their daughter and Dadai placed the mug carefully on the small table next to the rocking chair.

Echo glanced at the sofa, upon which the selkie skins were draped. She turned to her mother, puzzle pieces clicking together in her brain.

"You knew where they were hidden," she said.

"Yes, sweetheart," Mamai replied. "I've always known. They weren't hidden from me. They were hidden from you."

"But why?" Echo looked at the skins again. One large, one tiny. More pieces fell into place. "Is the small one mine?"

Her mother laid a gentle hand on her knee. "No."

Echo frowned as the pieces of the mystery unexpectedly changed shape. "Then...?"

"Runa, we have to start from the beginning," Dadai interrupted her.

Her mother nodded. "You tell the story, Gareth. You are the story-teller, after all."

Dadai's jaw worked. "Will she believe the tale if I tell it?" He caught Echo's gaze and held it, and she wanted to weep for the suffering she saw there, suffering she had inflicted with her words. She wanted to apologize, but there was still so much she did not understand. Echo held herself rigidly still, studying his face.

Dadai gave a weary shake of his head. "Your mother is right. It is time you heard the whole story. Long past time, I suppose."

Echo took a sip of the tea. Its calming warmth coursed through her, spreading out and soothing the wrenching guilt. She fixed her gaze on her father as he began his tale.

8

DADAI'S STORY

"*A*s you well know, I was not always a stevedore," Dadai began, leaning back into his chair. "In my youth, I worked on a merchant's ship. I wanted to explore the ocean, and I thought that would be a good way to see more of the world than I could in any other profession. I disappointed my father, I think. He hoped I would take after him, but I couldn't see myself working in the mill every day for the rest of my life, breathing in flour until I choked on it. I needed the sky above me and the sea around me. Eventually, I think he came to understand, though he was never happy about it.

"I saw the world, little wood-sprite! And the world was far vaster than I had imagined. I saved up the money from all my voyages, hoping to one day have enough to buy my own ship. I dreamed of sailing out into the ocean and away from the known trade routes. I wanted to discover something nobody else had found, set foot where no other man had walked. And one night, I got my wish, though not in the way I had expected.

"You know the story of my accident. There was a storm at sea. One minute I was up in the crow's nest, keeping a sharp eye out for rocks, and the next there was this sizzling flash of light and I was plunging into the icy cold water. The ropes were twisted around my leg, and the mast, which as you know had been struck by lightning and fallen overboard, was pulling me down into the depths. Luckily, I had my knife strapped to my ankle and I managed to cut the ropes away. Then I paddled and kicked as hard as I could, though it felt like my leg was on fire, but I couldn't find the surface. My lungs were screaming for air and I knew I was going to drown. But then something happened I did not expect. Something grabbed hold of me and pulled me up to the surface. That first breath of air when my head emerged was the sweetest thing I had ever tasted, but it also brought a surge of fear. I was in the middle of a stormy ocean all by myself. My ship was nowhere to be seen, and we were miles from any known land." He glanced at Mamai with a grin. "I think it was at that moment that I screamed."

Echo leaned forward, eager to know what happened next. Caught in the grip of a tale she had always yearned to hear, her anger diminished slightly. She had heard some of the rumors, but her father never spoke of the accident. As a small child, she had begged him to tell her about his last adventure at sea, but he always laughed and said, "Oh, you don't want to hear that story!"

Her father continued, "Then I felt something nudge its way under my arm, and I was surprised to find myself being held afloat by a seal, of all things! Then it began to swim. Through the wind and the waves and the storm, it kept my head above the surface. Finally, we reached the shore."

"It brought you home!" Echo breathed.

But Dadai shook his head. "No, I was much too far from Ennis Rosliath to swim there in one night."

"Then...?"

"To this day, I'm not sure where I slept that night, but in the morning, I could see that I was on a tiny island. I explored as best I could with my hurt leg and found a small spring of fresh water. I had nothing to make a fire, and I started to despair, thinking that I had been saved from drowning only to be brought to this isolated place to die. But just as I started to believe I would live out the rest of my very limited days on that island, the seal returned. It had brought me oysters." Dadai grimaced. "Not my favorite food, even cooked."

Echo wrinkled her nose.

"But I ate them, and gratefully." Dadai grinned, an echo of his old laughter gleaming in his eyes. "Mostly grateful that it wasn't raw fish."

Echo's eyes widened. She hadn't considered that possibility.

"When I had eaten all the oysters I could stomach, the creature barked at me and wriggled toward the water. It took me a while to understand, but eventually I realized that it was trying to coax me back into the sea. I had no choice but to trust it, this creature who had saved me from drowning and starvation, so into the water I went. The seal nuzzled under my arm as before, and once more it began to swim, towing me along, though this time I was able to be a bit less of a burden." He smiled at Mamai. "It went on like this for days. Swimming from island to island, none of which I had ever seen before, but every one possessed fresh water in some fashion. Sometimes the seal did not return for several days, and I passed the time by exploring. I do not have the time now to tell you of the adventures I had in those weeks, nor of the creatures I encountered." Dadai paused, catching Echo's eyes with his own. "You might not believe me, even if I did take the time to tell you. Much of what I saw on that voyage I had thought existed only in myths and legends."

Exhilarated butterflies danced in Echo's stomach and fluttered up her spine. She leaned forward, hanging on her father's every word.

"But eventually, I saw the cliffs of Ennis Rosliath on the horizon, and I rejoiced at the sight, for I knew I was almost home. When I finally crawled up on the sand, I was too over-come with emotion and weariness to even stand. I lay there on the shore, the ocean caressing my feet as though reluctant to give me up. I do not know how long I rested there before a few of the villagers found me and brought me the rest of the way home.

"As soon as I was strong enough, I went down to the shore with a bucket of fresh fish. I wanted to thank the crea-ture who had been so faithful a savior to me."

"Is that why you take fish down to the shore once a month?" Echo asked.

Her father smiled. "Yes. And no. There is more to it than that. Patience, my wood-sprite." He tapped his fingers on his knee for a moment, his face thoughtful as he found his place in the story once more. "I took the sign of my gratitude down to the sea: a bucket of fresh fish."

Echo grinned.

"Several seals arrived and accepted my offering, but I could not be certain that the one who had saved me was among them. I spent much of the next few weeks sitting in the sun down by the rocks. As I got stronger, I went for walks along the shore. The sea has always called to me, and even after my ordeal, I still felt drawn to it. One evening when I felt strong enough, I went climbing among the cliffs. I stepped on a loose boulder and nearly broke my leg as it rolled out from under me. But as I rose, my eye caught on something large and brown that had been stuffed beneath the rock. I was horrified when I picked it up and saw that it was a seal skin, and not just any seal skin—I recognized a soft, golden brown color and a pattern of faint reddish-brown splotches farther down its back. It was my seal. My first, angry thought was that someone had been killing the creatures, which, as you know, is against the law on Ennis Rosliath. But then I heard someone singing, the most beautiful voice I had ever heard. Quietly, I scrambled over the rocks until I caught a glimpse of the singer. It was a woman." Dadai paused and smiled up at his wife, then glanced at Echo. "It was your mother. Suddenly, I was aware of the seal skin I was still holding, and in a sudden burst of insight, I realized what I had in my hands. Though selkies are believed to be nothing more than a myth, my recent experience had opened my mind to the possibility that there might be more truth to the old tales than most realized."

"What happened next?" Echo asked. She scarcely dared to breathe, the story had ensnared her so completely.

"I approached the woman carefully, for I did not want to frighten her. To my relief, I saw that she was clad in a dress the color of seafoam."

Mamai tossed her head. "The idea that selkies wander about without clothes on is a myth. Or wishful thinking." She sniffed, but her eyes danced with laughter.

Dadai grinned. "'I believe this is yours,' I said, holding the skin out to her. She turned, fear in her brown eyes. But I placed it carefully on the ground and backed away. 'I do not know if it is true that anyone who finds a selkie's skin—for that is what I think you are—may hold the creature captive, but you have nothing to fear from me in that regard. I would never hold anyone against their will. Especially not someone to whom I owe my life.'

"She smiled and accepted the skin, which she laid down on the rock next to her before inviting me to sit. I did, and we talked for many hours, long after the sun had set. It was the beginning of a long and complicated courtship."

Echo glanced at her mother, whose eyes never left Gareth's face. Her own glowed with a gentle light of ardent love, and Echo could see the truth of her father's words reflected there.

"Is that part of the myth true, Mamai? If he had stolen the skin, would you have been his captive?"

"The legends are true, sweetling," Mamai replied. "Though it happens rarely. My people are extremely careful, and as your father has already told you, there are plenty of uninhabited islands available."

"Did you... want him to find it?" Echo asked in a flash of sudden insight.

Mamai gave her a quiet smile. "The month we spent together returning to Ennis Rosliath made me confident of his character. My family devised the test to be certain."

Echo's mouth fell open, aghast. "Knowing the consequences if they were wrong?"

"I could have refused the test, but then they would have refused their blessing," Mamai said. "And then if I had married your father, I would not have been allowed to return to the sea for anything shorter than the rest of my life."

Echo took this in, pondering it. She glanced at the two selkie skins. "But then, why did you keep this from me?" she asked after a long pause. "And if the little one isn't mine, whose is it?"

Mamai's eyes filled with tears and she turned away.

Dadai answered. "I am sorry, wood-sprite, but this is where we come to the part of the story that will be most difficult for you to hear. After your mother and I were married, I built her this house, where she could always be near the sea she loved. We knew it might be dangerous if anyone else knew her true nature, so we decided that she would only change form and return to the sea on stormy nights, when no prying eyes would be watching. Two and a half years after we were married, the Creator blessed us with a daughter. We named her Jana."

Echo frowned. Her parents had never told her about an older sister. Fear of the answer nearly kept her from asking, but the need to know proved stronger. "What happened to her?"

With a shuddering intake of breath, Mamai took over the story. "In those days, many infants were afflicted with a mysterious disease. You may have heard it called the wasting sickness, or the changeling sickness."

Echo nodded dumbly.

"Healthy babies would suddenly grow sickly and weak, then finally perish. No medicine could cure them, and no doctor could explain it," Mamai continued. "The mothers would swear that their child had been perfectly healthy, and some even went mad and refused to acknowledge that their child had died, claiming that their healthy baby had been replaced with a changeling by the fae." Mamai's eyes grew distant and sorrowful.

Gareth gazed at his wife with tender compassion. "When Jana was just a few months old, she was taken from us."

"By the disease?" Echo asked.

Dadai shook his head. "No. By the fae."

"But, I thought that... you said that the women who said that were mad."

"Aye," Mamai whispered. "That's what everyone thought. Even I believed it. Though I knew the fae were real, I couldn't see what use they would have for human children. But then, Jana disappeared." She bit her lip, then reached out and pulled Echo into a warm embrace. "You were left in her cradle."

Echo's body went stiff. Of all the things she had steeled herself to hear, this scenario had never appeared in even her wildest imaginings. Echo of the Fae. The words resounded through her thoughts and she shuddered violently, her head swinging back and forth in vicious denial.

"What?" She pushed herself away from her mother and sat back in the rocking chair, staring at her parents in bewildered hurt. "What are you saying?"

"Sweetling..." Mamai reached for her again, but Echo held up a hand.

"Don't," she choked. "Are you... are you saying I'm not your daughter?"

"Echo," Mamai said, hurt brimming in her eyes, but Echo couldn't help herself.

"Is that all I am to you?" she burst out, anger, hurt, and fear blending into a tornado within her. "An echo of your real daughter?" Hot tears streaked over her cheeks. She saw her mother wince, but in her own pain, she did not care.

"We would never say that," Dadai's voice thundered forcefully, and she could see that she had wounded him. "You are very much our daughter. We love you with every fiber of our beings, every bit as much as if you had been born to us."

Echo reeled, her thoughts whirling dizzily. "But... then... who am I?"

"You are our daughter," Mamai repeated.

The fierce love in their eyes was beyond doubt. It grounded her and she regretted the words she had flung like daggers. She took a deep breath and asked, in a calmer tone, "Who else am I?"

"We don't know," Mamai answered, her expression filled with a strange helplessness. "And we do not know what happened to Jana. You even looked like her, for a month or two. The fae can put a temporary glamour upon the things they enchant. The only reason we realized there had been a switch right away was that our baby suddenly had no affinity for her sealskin."

Echo's heart ached. Not only for herself, but also for her parents. What must they have gone through at that moment? To lose a child was bad enough, a pain she could not even imagine, but to lose their child in such a horrible way! And worse, to lose their child and not be able to even tell anyone, because nobody would be able to see the loss... a lump lodged itself in her throat.

"I journeyed deep into the Faeorn, determined to find our daughter," Dadai said, and Echo remembered their conversation from a few weeks ago. "I searched... oh, how I searched! I began by going to an old bridge deep in the forest."

Echo nodded, remembering how she had sat there earlier that same day, and how there had been a feeling of sleeping power in those ancient stones.

"Structures like that are often rumored to hide entrances into the faerie realm," her father continued, "but if there is a portal there, I never found it. I called out, begging, pleading, eventually mocking and berating the fae, anything to make them appear. I was willing to risk even their wrath if only it allowed me the chance to find my daughter, but they never came. Unlike your mother, I have no fae blood, and the realm of faerie remained closed to me."

"Is she still out there, somewhere, then?" Echo whispered.

"I don't know," Mamai replied, her voice soft, tears trailing down her cheeks. "We tried to find her. I asked my family for their aid, but they can do little against the land-fae in their own realm. And now"—she stared at her hands—"it is too late."

"Too late for what?" Echo asked.

"Jana's thirteenth birthday," Dadai replied. "Like you, she will turn thirteen in just over two weeks, on the first day of summer. If she is still alive..." he trailed off.

"Selkies cannot live long without the sea," Mamai explained in a soft, hopeless voice. "Especially once they reach adulthood. If Jana is still alive, she would need to return to the sea and transform before her birthday, or she will die anyway."

9

ECHO MAKES A DECISION

*E*cho lay in bed staring at the ceiling. Her head ached with the groggy nausea of mental exhaustion, and yet she could not sleep. Her parents' story left her marooned and panic-stricken. It was like that day on the rocks when the tide came in, sweeping around her and cutting her off from the shore. That terror that, at any moment, she might drown. Anger surged in her breast like the rolling tide: anger at the lies, anger at the fae, anger at the Creator for allowing all this pain. The anxious chorus in her mind never abated, so she didn't feel herself begin to doze. Sleep came fitful and stealthy, bringing her dark nightmares that flung her into consciousness shaking and terrified before receding just enough to lure her into sleep once more.

Morning brought a great sense of relief, and Echo left her bed like a wild thing fleeing its captors. The horizon shimmered with a slightly paler shade of navy, the only visible sign of night's reluctant departure. However, Echo could not bear to return to her bed for another second. Though she could not remember them, the faint recollection of dark dreams shivered throughout her slight frame.

Her parents were still asleep, so she quietly threw on her clothes, tiptoed outside, and took flight to the sweet, piney relief of the forest.

However, once she reached the trees, Echo found that she could not remain still. The peace that usually suffused her in the presence of the towering trunks and the gurgling brook eluded her. She tried to sit beneath her favorite tree, but found herself constantly springing back to her feet, filled with a nervous liveliness that made her pace restlessly. In the face of her frenetic energy, her forest friends did not show themselves, though one of the familiar squirrels scolded her from the safety of a lofty branch.

"What am I?" she wondered aloud, her voice soft and frustrated in her own ears. "Who am I?"

Tired of pacing, Echo began to wander. She had no destination in mind, and in fact barely looked up as she walked along, just needing to move, looking down at her toes as she kicked at small stones and leaves. She wished for some sort of purpose to guide her. An emptiness gaped inside, gnawing fretfully at her insides. The world she had understood had turned sideways and nothing felt right. She no longer fit anywhere. All her life, she had consoled herself with the fact that she nestled quite nicely into her place at home, but now she knew it had never been her home.

The sound of the chattering creek drew her attention from the ground and she paused, startled by where her feet had led her. She stood once more before the ancient bridge. Behind her, the first rays of dawn glimmered on the horizon. The little waterfall that gushed under and around the collapsed stones babbled cheerfully as it cast itself onto the rocks with joyful abandon.

Echo was reminded of a snatch of a poem she had once heard her mother recite:

> *Oh! How joyfully the waterfall*
> *Unchecking its course and flow*
> *Throws itself to the river below*
> *Over the jagged wall.*

It was true. The water feared nothing of the future or the course its winding banks might lead it to. It simply surged forward heedlessly. She crouched down on the bank of the creek, dabbling her fingers in the cool water.

What must it be like to have that kind of trust? she wondered idly. To care nothing for the future?

A glimmer at the corner of her vision distracted her and she pulled her gaze back to the bridge. She squinted, not trusting her own eyes. For there, spanning the two broken parapets, she could see a shimmering, golden outline of the bridge made whole.

Beyond that veil, the Faeorn looked different. The air fairly sparkled with life, and the colors around her intensified. The restored span seemed solid enough to walk on, and a sudden thrill shot through her. The anger and hurt of the evening before faded at this sudden revelation of the truth of her parents' words. The fae were real.

And she was one of them.

Her father had wandered these woods, and no door had ever opened for him, but for her... Her aimless restlessness coalesced into an iron resolve. What she had always denied and seen as a curse: her elfin looks, her affinity for the forest, the teasing words of her classmates... she might somehow use these things to right the terrible wrong. She could get into that world. She could search for her lost sister. If Jana lived, Echo could bring her home and save her life.

It startled her at first, to find that she thought of Jana as "sister," but in the next breath she realized that it also felt natural, something akin to comforting. Her own parentage was in no doubt. She may not have been born to the family she had, but she wished for no other. In spite of her initial hurt and confusion of the night before, in spite of the secrets they had kept concealed, her security in her parents' love for her was complete. The evidence of its existence, of its truth, was woven into the very fabric of her being. The revelation of Jana's existence could not threaten that love, only add to it.

Echo set her jaw. Scrambling along the bank of the river, she slowly made her way to the bridge. Her bare feet slipping on the stone steps, she stood upon the bridge, poised to step out onto the golden arch. Fear clutched at her heart, and she hesitated, thinking of her parents. If she disappeared, too, it would break their hearts. And besides, she did not know anything about the faerie realm, not even its name. She had heard a myriad of stories, however, and knew that the fae were cunning tricksters. An invitation this obvious might indicate a trap of some kind. Perhaps she should wait and consider her decision to cross the boundary between worlds; perhaps she should plan more carefully. But then, what if the doorway closed? What if she could not find another? Could one really plan to enter the faerie realm? She hung on the edge of indecision for a long moment, her foot poised to take a step.

Closing her eyes, she stepped forward, and felt her foot

come down on nothing but air. Her eyes flew open and she clutched at the crumbled railing, fighting to keep herself from tumbling over the broken segment of the bridge and down into the shallow, rocky creek below. The door had closed, rejecting her passage.

When she had pushed herself back to safety, she looked around, frowning. What had happened? The morning sun streamed through the trees behind her, mocking her attempt.

Had the doorway rejected her? Or had she simply hesitated for too long? She did not know, but seeing the vision of the faerie realm strengthened her resolve from a moment before. She would return and find a way into the faerie realm. She would rescue Jana and bring her home. But there were preparations she should make, and items she would need: a change of clothes, a blanket, food and water. And the tiny selkie skin! She added the item to her mental list. If Jana did not know her true identity, the skin might help convince her.

With determined strides, Echo left the forest and made her way home. The sun was now fully above the horizon, but the dew still hung fresh on the ground. When she reached the cottage, Runa looked like she might run out to meet her, but instead she greeted her with a tentative smile, and Echo answered by throwing her arms around her in a warm embrace.

"I love you, Mamai," Echo whispered fiercely.

Mamai's eyes filled with tears and she tightened her own arms around Echo. "I love you, too, darling," she whispered.

"Has Dadai left yet?"

"No," Mamai replied. "He went out to the barn to see if you were there. When we woke and found you gone, we didn't know what to think, and after everything last night...

he didn't want to leave for the docks until he had made sure you were all right."

Echo felt a flash of remorse. It had not occurred to her that her absence might be cause for worry, she had been so full of a need to move, to act.

"I didn't mean to worry you," Echo said, and explained her absence. "But I am glad he's still here. I... I have something I need to talk about with you both."

Mamai smoothed back Echo's hair and gave her a curious look, but did not press for details.

"Gareth," she called out the front door, "she's here. She's all right."

A few moments later, her father rushed into the house. When he saw Echo, he paused awkwardly, a wash of emotions—relief, worry, and uncertainty chiefest among them—crossing his face. Echo raced across the room and flung herself toward him.

"Dadai, I'm sorry!" She wrapped her arms around him, sobbing into his chest. "When I found the skins I... I lost my way. I didn't know what to think. I'm sorry I doubted you. I'm sorry I said such horrible things!"

Dadai held her, patting her back for a moment, then he pushed her away and gave her a serious look. "I am glad to know you no longer think I am a monster." He chuckled, but the weary, empty sound was devoid of all mirth.

"Our daughter wants to discuss something with us," Runa said, looking between them.

Gareth frowned. "Oh?"

Echo bit her lip, staring down at the floorboards for a long moment. Then she gathered her courage and looked up at her parents, meeting their eyes with all the confidence she could muster.

"I want to search for my sister."

Runa sat down at the table with a heavy thump. Gareth stared at Echo, his expression uncomprehending.

"You want to do what?" he asked.

"I want to search for my sister," Echo replied. "Jana," she added, in case they did not understand who she meant.

Mamai gave a quiet little sob.

"No..." Dadai drew the word out slowly. It didn't sound like he was forbidding her, more like it was the only thing he could think to say.

"I saw a doorway," Echo said, her words coming out in a disjointed rush, "a golden bridge, and on the other side, the forest looked different. I must be part fae. To be able to see the door, that's what it must mean, right? And then I knew I had to do it, to find her and bring her home."

Dadai held up his hands. "Slow down, little wood-sprite! Slow down. I'm not following you. Why don't you start at the beginning, and tell us everything." He drew her over to the table and they both sat down, joining her mother.

Echo took a deep breath and then started over, telling them everything, how she had slept poorly and woken early, how she hadn't wanted to disturb them and had fled to the forest, but found no comfort there, and eventually wandered to the bridge, which had opened to her presence. They listened patiently, not even asking any questions. When she finished, there was a long silence.

"Please," Echo said. "If Jana is alive, this could be our only chance to save her, to get her back."

"Absolutely not," Mamai whispered.

"Runa." Dadai put his hand over hers. "Wait."

"You cannot be seriously considering this!" Mamai exclaimed.

"Not sending her alone, no." Dadai shook his head. "But if the doorway between realms opens for her, perhaps I can go with her."

Mamai considered this. Hope and relief fluttered in Echo's chest. If Dadai went with her, surely they would succeed.

"You cannot have given up all hope, Runa," Dadai whispered. "Not yet. There is still time…"

"Very well," Mamai said at last, her voice trembling. "It is worth a try. Of course it is worth a try." She pressed her lips into a determined line, but a beacon of fear shone from her eyes, pooling with tears.

10

JOURNEY INTO THE FAEORN

*I*t took a few hours to pack their provisions for the journey into the Faeorn. Blankets, changes of clothes, flint and steel, food, the selkie skin wrapped carefully and lying at the bottom of Echo's pack. They had decided to enter the forest at twilight, when the border between worlds was supposed to be weakest. If they could not find the doorway, Echo and her father would camp in the forest for a few days to see if it might return.

Mamai fussed over each of them, checking and rechecking their packs until Echo thought she might burst with impatience. She knew her mother wanted to join them, but her connection to the sea made it too dangerous for her to enter the faerie realm. But at last, there was nothing left to check, and Mamai pulled Echo into her arms.

"My heart aches for Jana," she whispered into Echo's ear, "but her loss brought us you, and to undo that gift would shatter my heart forever." She held Echo by the shoulders, gazing into her eyes with deep gravity. "So you had better come home when this is all over."

Echo found that she could not speak, and so she simply nodded, her heart too full for words.

Gareth kissed his wife goodbye. "We will be back by the first day of summer," he promised. "I'll bring her home safely."

Mamai used the edge of her apron to wipe her eyes, then she sniffed once and lifted her chin, smiling bravely. She waved at them as they left, standing in the doorway of the cottage. Echo kept glancing over her shoulder to look back at her mother, so strong and yet forlorn. She waved one last time as they crested the first rolling hill, and then they descended down through the field on the other side and the cottage and her mother disappeared from sight.

They hiked in silence across the fields. At the edge of the Faeorn, as if by some unspoken agreement, they paused and stared into its depths. Echo felt a shiver scuttle up her spine. The Faeorn had always been a respite for her, a place of comfort and peace. But now, the shadows seemed longer, the trees swayed ominously, as though warning her against entering the wood. She found herself feeling adrift, as if returning from a long voyage to find her home inhabited by strangers and all familiar furnishings removed.

"Shall we?" She jumped at her father's quiet voice that sounded too loud in her ears.

Echo swallowed with an effort and nodded. Her heart thudded in her head and apprehension tingled in her veins. Her imagination conjured up a vision of the trees reaching out and tearing her away from her father and crushing the air from her lungs. As he began to take a step into the forest, Echo reached out and slipped her small hand into her father's larger one, holding him back. He stopped and looked down at her, misgiving written across his features.

"Echo?"

"It's nothing." She forced a small laugh. It sounded nervous and thin to her own ears. "I just don't want to lose you in there."

He squeezed her hand. "You and me both! Together, then?"

She nodded. Taking a deep breath, the two of them ventured into the Faeorn.

A warm breeze ruffled their hair, and the leaves rustled as they walked. They talked a little as they went, their voices hushed, not quite whispering.

"How are you doing?" Dadai asked.

Echo pondered the question, stepping over a large tree root jutting from the ground. She had barely had time to process anything, but to her surprise, she did not feel much different from how she always felt.

"I'm all right," she replied at last. "Truly."

"I know it's a lot to take in."

"Yes. At first I felt a little"—she strained to find the right words— "adrift. Finding out about Jana was... difficult. But then I started thinking about you and Mamai and, oh, just everything, and I realized that it doesn't really change anything."

"It doesn't?" Her father sounded genuinely surprised.

Echo shook her head. "No. Because I'm still me. I'm still your daughter. You can't erase thirteen years just by saying it wasn't what you thought it was. Does that make sense?" She felt herself stumbling over her thoughts, flailing to express them in a way that he could understand. "I guess what I'm trying to say is... I'm... thankful." She paused, startled by her own revelation, but as she examined it, she found it to be true and pure, a small nugget of gold she would tuck away as precious.

"Thankful?"

"To be your daughter. And to discover I have a... sister." She offered a tentative smile, which he returned with a radiance like the dawning sun.

The forest loomed over them, commanding their reverence and whispering of foul fates and lost souls. Echo shivered, wrapping her arms around herself.

"Are you cold?" Dadai asked.

"No. It's just..." Echo glanced up at the trees, her heart heavy. "I'm not used to feeling unwelcome here."

Dadai put his arm around her shoulders and pulled her against his side. "I don't think it's you that is unwelcome."

A stinging sensation developed behind the bridge of her nose and she hugged him back fiercely, trying to put all her love and admiration into the embrace. The Faeorn's coldness toward them hurt; the betrayal was a physical ache in the center of her chest. If only she could show the forest her father the way she saw him, she knew it would have no choice but to embrace him as well. But she did not know how to put words to that sentiment.

Dadai ruffled her hair, though not enough to muss it. "I'm not hurt by it, little wood-sprite," he assured her.

They reached the ancient stone bridge and Echo climbed the crumbling steps. But no golden aura appeared. A heavy weight of disappointment settled in the pit of her stomach.

"It's gone," she said thinly. "It was here... Do you see anything?"

"No," Dadai replied. "But don't worry; what you saw happened at dawn, a time when the barriers between worlds are naturally weakened. We will wait until twilight and see if it happens again."

"What if it doesn't?"

"Then we will camp here and wait until morning, and if nothing happens then, we'll find a new place to look."

Echo heaved a sigh and descended from the bridge. She helped her father set up their little campground, rolling out their blankets, digging a small pit, and gathering dead wood for a tiny fire; the nights were still cool and they might need a source of warmth once the sun set. After that, there was nothing left to do but wait. Echo passed the time by tossing pebbles into the little creek and watching them splash. She wished she could introduce her woodland friends to her father, but she was too restless to sit still and wait for their appearance, and she did not think she could bear the disappointment if they spurned her on account of her father. When she grew bored with throwing rocks, she returned to their little campsite and tried to pass some more time rearranging her blanket.

Dadai was rifling through his pack looking for something, but then he stopped, a strange smile playing about the corners of his mouth.

"Look what your mother did," he said, drawing out the little stick puppets and handing one to her.

Echo clapped her hands in delight and sat down next to him, holding the little figure her father had fashioned for her when she was younger. Warmth and contentment spread through her entire body and she drew her knees up to her chest, clasping her hands around them.

"Want a story?"

"Will you tell me the story about Moses again, Dadai?" she asked. "The one where his mother put him in a basket?"

Dadai's eyes softened. "Are you wondering about your own mother?"

Echo dropped her gaze, muffling her words in her knees. "I don't... I... maybe," she admitted.

"I wish I could tell you something... anything about her," Dadai sighed. "I have often wished I knew who she was, so that I could thank her for the gift she gave us that night when she brought you to us. I would like to be able to show her what a fine young lady her daughter has grown into."

"I'm glad she left me with you!" Echo's vehemence surprised her as suddenly the words flowed out. "I don't care who she was or why she gave me up... I love you and Mamai... but... she gave me to you. I guess... I guess I should feel angry with her... but... I don't. I love you and Mamai so much, I just can't be mad at her, I can only be thankful. She gave me the best parents I could ever have asked for."

Dadai's eyes glistened with a sudden silvery sheen. In a choked voice he said, "That day when we discovered the change... it was a hard day. Losing a child is never easy. It shouldn't be easy. But we had you, and we knew you had been put in our lives for a reason. I have never questioned that the Creator brought you to us."

Echo leaned against him. "Just like Moses and the Pharaoh's daughter."

Dadai cleared his throat and lifted up one of the puppets. "Pharaoh feared the great nation his slaves had become, and so he gave the order that any baby boys among the Hebrews should be killed. One brave woman decided to hide her infant son, and so she placed him in a woven basket and hid him in the tall plants along the shore of the river and left his sister to watch over him."

Her father used the puppets as he always did, affecting

their different voices and bringing the familiar story to life. As it unfolded, Echo thought of Moses' mother, who had given up her son for someone else to raise, knowing it was the only way to save his life. Her courage and love had never struck her so forcefully before, and she marveled at that ancient woman's strength. She wondered what had prompted her own mother, what had prompted her to place her infant daughter in that cradle. Had she been in danger? Had she felt unable to care for her own child? Or had something else been the cause of her sacrifice?

Dusk fell, but the golden bridge did not manifest. Echo and her father ate their supper in silence. While darkness engulfed them, Gareth lit the little fire.

"Don't lose heart," he said quietly. "We still have time."

Echo nodded, but her hope fluttered uncertainly. The time they had was so fleeting. But she curled up under her blanket, wishing for her own bed and her cozy quilt. Echo watched the glowing embers of the fire flicker like magic until she slowly drifted off to sleep.

In the silver-gray light of predawn, Echo woke, roused by something she could not put words to. It was as though someone had called her name, but not out loud. Rather, something invisible tugged at her spirit. She sat up, completely alert, as though she had already been awake for hours. She looked around. The fire had died in the night, though some of the coals still radiated a little heat. Her father still slept soundly, his blanket pulled up around his chin.

The tug came again, gentle but insistent. Echo rose to her feet and quietly left the campsite, her bare feet padding silently over the forest floor. A moment later, she found herself standing at the foot of the stone bridge. Carefully, she climbed the steps and stared down.

The bridge stood whole and unbroken, the arch an opalescent gold in the gray light, just like before.

She had already started to turn, ready to shout for her father, when movement on the other side of the bridge caught her attention. As she watched, a woman climbed up the opposite flight of steps and came to stand in the center of the bridge, right where it normally appeared broken.

The hem of her flowing, twilight-hued gown brushed the gleaming line between Echo's ordinary stone stairway and the shining one. The woman had long black hair and slender, pointed ears. Her face seemed to glow with a silver light and she raised a delicate finger to her lips.

"Echo," she whispered, and the word rang through the air with the force of a command. "Do not call the human."

Fear shuddered through her. "How do you know my name?"

The fae—for she could only be a fae—smiled. "You are the first from the mortal realm to enter our forest without fear in many years. You have not escaped our notice."

Echo stopped at that, stunned. The Faeorn. Of course.

"Well, why shouldn't I call for my father?" she demanded, fear making her bold.

"Because if he awakens, all this will vanish. The Faerthain is not for mortal eyes. He will never be allowed to pass over the golden bridge and into our realm. If you wish to find the one you seek, you will have to leave him behind."

Echo's mouth turned to ash. "He will not understand. He will search for me. It will break his and Mamai's hearts if I disappear."

The woman shrugged. "If you insist on trying to bring him, your quest will fail."

Echo narrowed her eyes at the woman. "Why should I trust you?"

The fae-woman did not hesitate. She stepped closer and put her lips to Echo's ear. "My true name is Malilia."

Echo's eyes widened. "Are the stories true?" she breathed. "Does the knowledge of a fae's true name give the bearer power over them?"

Malilia gave a somber nod. "Some. Not as much as the stories say, but the giving of a true name is a symbol of trust."

"Why would you trust me so readily?" Echo asked, still suspicious.

This time Malilia did hesitate. "Because you are my daughter."

THROUGH THE PORTAL

A shock rippled through Echo's consciousness. "I... what... my... my mother?" Suspicion and disbelief coursed through her.

Malilia stepped back, eyes downcast. "Yes." Then she looked up, alarm flashing across her delicate features. "The sun is rising. The doorway will close soon. If you wish to come with me, I will do what I can to give you aid and answer your questions, but you must come now."

Still reeling but pervaded by a sense of urgency, Echo glanced back to where her father was still sleeping. If she wanted to rescue her sister, it had to be in this moment; she understood without asking that the offer of assistance would not be presented again.

With light footsteps, she dashed back to the campsite. Her movements hurried, she took her father's lantern and clipped it to her own pack before shouldering the entire contraption. Bending down, she brushed her lips against her father's cheek.

"Forgive me, Dadai," she whispered. "I will do everything

in my power to come home, and to bring Jana with me. I promise." She rose and stepped away, her bare feet whispering through the pine needles covering the forest floor.

Quickly, she climbed the bridge once more and stood at the border between realms. Malilia held out her hand. Somewhere on the horizon, the first rays of sunlight began to burst over the edge of the world as Echo reached across and gripped the woman's hand, quickly stepping through the fading portal.

A shudder of cold. A wrenching sensation, as though the world were being drawn through her entire being. And then she found herself blinking on the other side of the barrier, her eyes struggling to adjust. They still stood on a bridge in a wood, but everything else was different. The bridge itself was no longer weathered stone, but a beautiful span of logs, perfectly split and hewn to fashion a smooth archway across a wide, flowing river. A delicate trailing vine with tiny, nearly translucent white flowers trimmed the edges of the railing. From there, Echo began to realize that it wasn't only the bridge; everything was different. Every trunk, leaf, and pine needle was limned in golden sunlight; even the colors had intensified. The trees here were much taller than those she had left behind; they towered above her, their great branches stretching to the sun in verdant magnificence. Because of their great girth and spread, the forest felt thinner than it had a moment ago, for trees such as these could not grow so closely together. Panic welled up within her as she whirled around, grasping for anything familiar.

"Where am I?" she breathed, though in her heart she knew the answer.

"Welcome to Faerthain," Malilia said, spreading her arms.

"Aren't we still in the Faeorn, though?"

Malilia smiled. "The Faeorn is merely our front door, the tiny fragment of our realm that exists in both the mortal and fae worlds. This is our realm: everything beyond the mighty River Perifell belongs to the fae and is part of Faerthain."

A squirrel skittered down the nearest tree and chattered at her. Echo smiled as she recognized her friend from the forest. Digging into her pouch, she pulled out a broken piece of honey cake and extended it to him. He snatched it and began nibbling on a corner.

"I didn't think I would see any familiar faces on this side of the door," Echo said.

"Animals can cross over as they wish," Malilia said. "But come, we must leave the bridge."

"Why?"

"The queen's guards will have felt your crossing and will be here soon to investigate."

"Is that bad?"

Malilia hesitated. "It is not ideal," she said, appearing to choose her words carefully.

A shout reached their ears and Malilia's face drained of color.

"Quickly, follow me!" she hissed, darting into the underbrush.

Echo hesitated for the briefest instant, then followed at a run, but she'd already lost sight of the woman. She whirled about, feeling panic setting in. Golden helmets glinted in the sunlight as a troop of soldiers wound through the trees toward the bridge. She wanted to cry out to her guide, but fear closed her throat, as she knew that any sound she made would only alert the guards to her presence.

A hand shot out from behind a tree and pulled her around into a little hollow between two enormous buttress roots. She nearly screamed, but Malilia's face appeared before her own, the woman's eyes wide with fear as she pressed a finger to her lips. Echo gulped and sank to the ground, her heart pounding loudly in her ears.

Voices drifted on the breeze, though she could not make out the words. Cautiously, she stood and peered over one of the roots, straining her eyes. Five soldiers stood about the bridge, their plate mail gleaming silver in the sunshine. One, with his sword drawn, pointed at the bridge insistently. The other men dutifully checked the expanse and then fanned out, searching the surrounding area.

"They can't have gone far!" the leader shouted.

One of the guards paused a hand's breadth from their hiding place and Echo's heart pounded wildly. Surely he must hear it! But a moment later, he moved on.

The guards continued to expand their perimeter, and eventually moved out of sight.

Malilia sighed and rose, brushing dirt and leaves from her long skirt. "Come," she whispered.

"How...?" Echo wanted to ask a hundred questions, but Malilia raised her finger to her lips once more.

"Not here," the woman said, her tone hushed. "Wait." Then she darted into the forest, beckoning for Echo to follow her.

Echo watched her go, for the moment caught in equivocation. This was not at all how she had envisioned her quest proceeding. Of course, she had planned on being here with her father. She had not expected the faerie realm to be quite so hostile and mysterious. But Jana's time was running out; this might well be the only chance she would ever have to reunite her family.

With a shrug and a whimper she tried to quell, she shouldered her pack and followed her guide, moving quickly through the enormous trees. Echo struggled to keep up with the gliding paces of the fae, her pack pulling on her shoulders and the lantern banging against her leg uncomfortably when she was forced to jog. As they went, her mind had time to process, and questions began to bubble to the surface of her thoughts, but she sensed that Malilia wanted her to wait a bit longer; the fae woman... her mother... certainly seemed to have a destination in mind.

Eventually, after walking several miles, Malilia reached a tree and began to ascend, gliding up and around the massive bole. Echo paused, her mouth agape, partially to catch her breath and partially from incredulity. She was about to ask how she could follow when she noticed the clever stairs cut into the wood. Carefully, not quite trusting the structure, she hefted her bag and began to climb. The steps were tiny and Echo had to grip the edges with her bare toes, but eventually she made it to the top, where she found a door carved into the trunk.

"Hello? Malilia?" she called in a quavering voice. Had the woman forgotten she was there? All the stories said the fae were flighty, capricious creatures. Had the woman simply grown bored with what had only been an elaborate diversion all along?

The door swung inwards, and Malilia appeared, an apologetic smile on her face. "Forgive me; I left the door open, but the wind must have pushed it shut. Please, come in. We will be safe here."

Echo ducked into the dwelling and paused, stunned. Either the tree was larger than it looked from the outside, or considerable magic was at work. The walls were rough hewn from hollowing out the tree; a spiral stair in the center of the room wound up around a column of wood. A window she had not noticed from outside admitted a cool breeze and the gentle sounds of rustling leaves. Carved furniture was tastefully arranged throughout the home.

She shook herself out of her astonishment and decided the time for questions had come. "Is this your home?"

Malilia gave her a thoughtful look. "Not as such."

Echo pondered the answer, but the most intelligent response she could think of was, "What?"

"We fae don't have the same concept of 'home' as humans do. This is one of my retreats, but if I am not here, then others may use it freely."

"Then how is it safe? And what did you mean by that? I did not come here to hide, I came here to find my sister and bring her home."

"I meant that the guards have passed beyond this area and that they would not think to look in a fae haven. As for your sister, I will do what I can to help you," Malilia said. "But there are things you must know first."

"Like what?" Echo demanded, her patience giving out. "I think the first thing I need to know is: who are you? You say you're my mother, but what proof do I have of that? And either way, why should I trust you? If the guards are looking for you, then keeping your company seems like a bad idea. I need to find my sister, and she doesn't have much longer. So tell me why I shouldn't climb down this tree and let you deal with your own problems!"

"The guards aren't looking for me, they are looking for you," Malilia snapped. "You are the intruder here. How were you planning on getting past them on your own? And even if you could avoid them, how exactly do you hope to find this sister of yours? Did you plan to wander the whole of

Faerthain shouting her name? Would you even recognize her if you saw her?"

The enormity of her own lack of preparation crashed over her like the driving rain of a storm. Embarrassed, Echo wilted into a chair, her energy sapped. For the first time in her life, she knew what loneliness was. It was helplessness and insignificance and knowing that nobody would come. Alone, she would be lost to the wind and the tide; the world would keep on heedlessly turning, unconcerned by her meager plight. If only her father could have come with her! She eyed the fae woman with a spark of weary suspicion.

"How do I know I can trust you?" she asked again.

Malilia's dark eyes turned gentle. "I gave you my true name."

"I've spent my entire life in the mortal realm. Just because I've heard stories about commanding the fae doesn't mean I have any idea how to do it. And you must know that, so it wasn't really any risk. So..." She settled in her chair, trying for belligerence but probably only managing pitiful. "Why should I trust you?"

Malilia sighed and slumped into a seat nearby. "I do not expect you to believe me, but I only wish to undo the harm I caused thirteen years ago."

Echo leaned forward, a fiery prick of resentment and anger burning through her heart. She wondered why it had never occurred to her that her mother, who had left her with Gareth and Runa McIntyre, must also have been responsible for stealing Jana away. Perhaps she hadn't wanted to be forced to think of the woman who bore her as the thief that tore her family apart. In her mind, she had almost been able to completely separate the two events, but now the truth rushed over her in all its stark clarity.

"Why?" she whispered.

Malilia gave a bitter laugh. "It is the perfect question. Why? Why did I do it? Why do the fae take mortal children? Why did I leave you behind? It is all part of the same question, and all has the same answer, but I do not know if you will be able to understand. Besides, it is a long story."

Echo set her pack on the floor beside her chair with a thump. "I'm listening."

12

MALILIA'S TALE

*M*alilia stared at a spot on the wall above Echo's head. "The queen wanted a child," she began. "Queen Titania and King Oberon can't have children, you know."

Echo shook her head. How could she know that? These names were foreign to her.

"No, I suppose you wouldn't know. The mortals have their stories, of course, and many of them hit near the mark, but this is a secret the king and queen keep to themselves. Even among the fae it is not common knowledge."

"How do you know about it, then?" Echo could not refrain from asking.

Malilia smiled sadly. "I am one of Queen Titania's personal attendants, part of her inner circle. Every time she was struck with that feverish need for a child, we were dispatched to find one for her. The fae don't have many children to begin with, so our search often took us into the mortal realm."

"The changeling sickness," Echo whispered.

"Yes." Malilia's face darkened. "We would fashion babies out of whatever our gifts worked best with—mud, sticks, flowers, rocks—and glamour them to look like a living child. Then, Titania provided us with a powerful magic, a gift that allowed us to create an illusion of life around it. We would leave behind that glamoured doll in the cradles of the mortal children we spirited away."

"Stole, you mean," Echo interjected hotly.

A pained expression lined Malilia's face. "Yes," she whispered. "Stole." She heaved a sigh. "No matter what we did, even the most beautiful of our creations soon faded, leaving the mortal women under the belief that their baby had sickened and died. We brought the babies to our queen, presenting them to her so that she could choose an heir. But none of them ever truly captured her fancy. They were not special enough, they cried too much, or she thought them too ugly, too smelly, or just too... mortal." Malilia's shoulders drooped. "I stole many babies away from their mothers, trying to please my queen. We all knew that whoever could bring her an heir would earn her eternal favor.

"This went on for many years, though sometimes several years would pass before the longing struck Titania again. I must confess, I relished the challenge of it: stealing into a mortal's home undetected, the thrill of bringing yet another option to my queen... I looked forward to the years when the longing would strike her."

Echo's soul shriveled with every word the woman said. She wanted to leap up and shake her, scream at her, demand to know how she could have enjoyed bringing such pain to so many.

Malilia caught her eyes and her face contorted in shame, as though she could read the revulsion in Echo's thoughts.

"For long turnings of the seasons and equally long sorrows, I have wished I could take back those years," she whispered brokenly. She stared down at her hands resting in her lap. "What I wouldn't give to undo all of it." She no longer seemed to remember that Echo was in the room.

"Why didn't Titania just demand a fae child?" Echo asked. "Why steal human babies?"

Malilia kept her eyes downcast. "To steal from her own subjects... would be unthinkable. The queen does not... esteem humans... in the same way."

"What changed?" Echo asked hoarsely.

Malilia glanced up. "You did." She gave a soft smile. "Or rather, you changed me. Thirteen years ago, I had you. When I held you in my arms... I... I can't explain it. I can't describe it. There are no words for the love I felt. It was sudden, unexpected, and irreversible. And as suddenly as it came, it brought the full realization of what I had done crashing down upon me. When Titania called us to her and commanded once more that we find her a child, I knew I couldn't... I couldn't do what I had done for so many years. I couldn't steal another woman's joy. Those mortal women became real to me, and I knew that it was wrong.

"But to defy Titania, or to return empty-handed... both were out of the question. I wandered through the mortal realm, carrying you with me, like someone lost. I did not know what to do. My footsteps led me out onto the beach, and I saw a young couple, rocking their newborn child to sleep in a cradle floating on the water. There was such love in their faces, such tenderness toward each other and the babe. And then I caught a glimpse of the child: her fluffy, fiery hair, and an aura that was undeniably faerie. I knew in that moment that if any child in the world could please Titania, it was that one. But I could not bring myself to leave behind another illusion that would fade to death and break those good people's hearts." Malilia's eyes filled with tears. "And so, when night fell, I kissed you and covered you in a glamour to resemble the child I... stole... and left you in her place. It ripped out my heart to leave you, but I had no choice. The only acceptable repayment for what I was stealing had to be the thing I treasured most."

Silence filled the little house, the only sounds those of the forest outside drifting in through the open window. Echo shifted uncomfortably, suddenly shy.

"Her father figured out my deception. He came into the Faeorn, wild with grief and desperation. I watched him as he searched for a way into Faerthain. I listened as he shouted out his rage, knowing I deserved every word. The glamour I had covered you with was intended for mortal children; I did not realize it would fade so quickly on one of our own. I believed your parents would never know the difference. But they did." Malilia's brow furrowed in confusion. "I never did quite understand how my magic faded so quickly. I had so wanted to spare them that pain. Too late, I understood that I had broken more than just my own heart."

"What happened to her? Jana?" Echo asked in a tiny voice, suddenly afraid of the answer.

Malilia took a long, shaky breath. "Queen Titania fell instantly in love with her. Jana was such a pleasant baby, and beautiful. She rarely cried or even fussed. Everything seemed to fill her with wonder; even when she was still an infant, she would gaze about with her wide, green eyes, smiling at everything. She smiled so early! Titania didn't even object when I suggested that she should be allowed to retain the name her mortal parents had given her. I had never seen the queen so enamored with a child, and I have never seen her so amiable! She fussed over her and doted on the child, refusing to delegate even diaper changes to any of her attendants. I watched her carefully, ever vigilant for any sign that her interest might wane, but it never did. Jana is the perfect Summer Princess, and Queen Titania adores her as much as ever. I comforted myself for the next several years, reminding myself that my sacrifice brought an end to the practice of stealing mortal children. Then you started wandering into the forest. I watched you when I could. It was clear that you were loved, even though I knew your parents had figured out my deception. Even though I knew I could never speak to you, I enjoyed getting to see you grow."

"I knew I was being watched," Echo muttered. She frowned. "But... why did you help me cross the barrier? You knew I was here to bring Jana home; why risk everything when the queen is finally happy with her heir?"

"The Summer Princess has fallen ill," Malilia replied.

Echo's stomach clenched. "What do you mean, ill?"

"It started at the end of last summer," Malilia said. "Jana began to experience headaches. At first they were just nuisances, but they have worsened over time. Then she began having nightmares, terrible nightmares that left her barely able to breathe, choking like her lungs had frozen. Most recently, she has had periods of time when she grows feverish and descends into a fitful state, not recognizing anyone, not even Oberon and Titania. At times she drifts about like one walking in her sleep, completely heedless of dangerous situations. The queen fears she is dying. After she nearly drowned the second time by wandering deliriously into the river, they had her placed in a high tower with no door in order to protect her. Every healing potion has been tried, every magical remedy essayed, all to no avail."

Echo listened to this with increasing agitation. "It is because she is half selkie!" she burst out. "If she doesn't return to the sea by the first day of summer and make the transformation, she will die! I have to take her home. Surely the queen would let me save Jana's life if she loves her so much. If you take me to Titania, I can explain it to her, I can show her the proof!"

Malilia's eyes widened at the outburst. "Selkie!" she breathed. "Of course! I knew she was part-fae, but I never could figure out what her specific heritage was. The sea-fae are not a part of Faerthain; they have their own realm."

"Then you will help me? You will take me to Titania?"

"No!"

"But why?" Anger resurfaced in Echo's voice. "You said yourself..."

"Titania will never believe you. She is distraught with grief over her daughter's illness and has gone half-mad already."

"But surely if she knew how simple the remedy was..."

"You do not understand. The sea-fae... it... there is history there you do not know, cannot comprehend. Titania will refuse to accept this news. Had I known, I would have left Jana in her own cradle and found another child to bring to my queen."

Echo sat back, stunned. She had no response to this. "Then... what should I do? If she stays here she won't survive. I have to save her!"

Malilia nodded. "I know. You will have to get into the tower and somehow bring the princess out and take her back to the mortal realm and the sea. And you do not have long to do it."

"I have just under two weeks," she said. "Can you take me to the tower?"

"I can..." Malilia hesitated. "But you should know: in the mortal realm you have two weeks. Here, it's closer to one."

"What?"

"Time passes differently in Faerthain."

"I see." And she did. The fluid nature of faerie time was common knowledge; it just hadn't occurred to her that this difference would ever affect her. The enormity of her task settled about Echo's shoulders. Had she been standing, it would have pushed her to her knees.

"What do I do?" she whispered.

"I will show you where she is kept," Malilia said. "You will be better able to plan your next steps once you see it."

Echo nodded numbly. She was just a child—with no more than her name and the contents of her pack. How in this strange, unknown land was she supposed to outwit and steal from the queen of the fae? And what if Jana refused to accompany her?

"What would the guards have done with me?" she asked, suddenly remembering the bridge and their flight through the forest.

"It is difficult to say for certain," Malilia replied darkly. "They might have simply sent you back to the mortal realm, but you could also have been dragged before Titania and Oberon."

"And what would they do with me?"

Malilia shrugged. "Most likely? Thrown you in a dungeon. Or, if they were feeling particularly generous, assigned you an impossible task. If you finished by the appointed deadline, you would be allowed to stay in Faerthain for as long as you liked."

"If not?"

"You would be summarily executed."

"Even if I was welcomed by one of the fae?" Echo asked.

"I did not have their permission to bring you here. If we are caught, I will share your fate."

Malilia let the silence hang off the end of her words. Echo swallowed, trying to muster some bravery. *Mamai, Dadai, will I ever see you again? Did I find the way to Jana only to break your hearts a second time?* She could feel tears pressing at the corners of her eyes, but she mastered them.

"Come along, the tower is some distance from here."

"Oh." Echo shivered. A terrible thought occurred to her. "What if we run into a patrol?"

"Despite living in the mortal realm your entire life, you are still a fae," Malilia said. "One reason I brought you to this house was so that we could speak in private and I could answer your questions, but the other reason was to cleanse you of the smell of mortality. If we run into a patrol, they will not be able to discern that you are anything other than one of the many fae who inhabit this realm. And a low-level one, at that, thanks to your clothes. They will not give you a second glance. One of our more powerful races might still sense it, but the guards will no longer be a problem."

Echo resisted the urge to sniff her arm, but she wondered what "mortality" smelled like. It did not seem like the sort of thing that had a smell, but she did not like to contradict her guide. Her mother. It was strange and unsettling, applying such a significant word to a total stranger.

She stood and shouldered her pack once more. "Lead the way."

13

A TERRIBLE TRUTH

*O*utside, the sun shone brilliantly down from a cloudless sky—Echo had never seen such a perfect azure before. Tiny, brightly-colored birds flitted above them as Malilia led her through the forest. As they hiked, the trees began to thin and grow noticeably smaller, until they had exited the forest altogether.

Now, Echo found herself on the edge of an enormous garden, but it was unlike any she had ever before encountered. It held no orderly rows of turnips and potatoes, no cabbage or rutabagas. Instead, this garden grew in wild tumblings of flowers and ferns, appearing at first glance to be rampantly overgrown and neglected. But as they ventured deeper into its pathways, Echo saw that there was a fierce sort of order. Roses of every color climbed delicate trellises that arched over the path at intervals, creating mystical bowers. Here and there she spotted benches nestled into nooks carefully preserved between short fir trees with their long, soft needles. The entire place, she realized, had been cultivated to give the semblance of chaos, and yet everywhere she looked she could see the signs of a careful gardener with an eye toward a pleasant experience for every visitor, whether they came for a romantic stroll, a secret tryst, or simply a quiet reading spot.

Do the fae read books? Echo wondered suddenly, and voiced the question before she had time to consider whether or not it might be rude.

"We don't read about life; we live," Malilia replied. "And we learn, not from reading, but from living."

"That's beautiful," Echo said. "And yet... hollow."

Malilia arched an eyebrow. "Hollow? What is in your books that is so wonderful?"

"Everything!" Echo enthused, warming to the topic. "Why, in books you can be anyone, go anywhere. There's a freedom to reading unlike anything else. When you read, it makes you think differently about the world and your own life, and sometimes it helps you understand what's going on around you by showing you a different perspective. And... well... there's beauty to be discovered in books, more real and more true because it's only limited by your own imagination. And besides, it's.... it's just... fun!"

Malilia grew thoughtful. "This is something you care about."

"Yes." Echo felt a little embarrassed. She did not usually speak so forcefully. "I like reading."

"I can tell." Malilia's eyes twinkled with amusement.

"What is this place?" Echo asked.

Malilia gave a distracted glance about them. "Oh, just one of the fae gardens."

"There are more like this?"

"Not identical, no," Malilia answered with the air of one not quite certain why she is having a particular conversation.

"There are different designers and each has their own unique flair."

"Then... this one doesn't have a name?"

"Naming things is a human trait."

"Then how do you know where to meet someone if they invite you to this particular garden?"

A flicker of amusement hovered about the faerie's lips. "This is the garden near the Faeorn."

"Huh." Echo gave a grunt of disappointment. "Seems to me a place like this should have a better name."

Malilia's eyes twinkled, but then she paused, her gaze taking in the scenery around them. "You know... perhaps you're right."

When they reached the other end of the garden, Echo sighed. She would have liked to linger and explore more of it. Thoughts of Jana propelled her forward, however, and she continued to traipse after Malilia out into the open countryside.

Over the next few hours, the landscape turned into rolling hills that led them past valleys full of shimmering, hidden lakes. They talked a little as they walked, Echo blurting questions as they occurred to her, but her uneasiness at speaking gradually waned as the faerie woman seemed neither perturbed nor amused by her awkward attempts at conversation. She still did not know what to think of this woman who had spent years stealing children. Her repentance seemed genuine, but the stories all agreed that the fae were capricious and changeable. And what had happened to all those children Titania had rejected? More than a few had never been returned to their families, of that she was certain. She kept her guard up as they walked, studying her guide warily.

Upward. Ever upward they climbed through the hills until finally, well past lunchtime, they reached the summit, and Echo thought she must be seeing the whole of Faerthain spread out below. Nestled against a larger hill rose a gleaming, ivory palace with silver turrets stretching gracefully into the sky. On either side, Echo could see a thick forest spreading away and around the slope like a retinue of guards and ladies-in-waiting attending the palace itself.

"That is where we must go," Malilia said, pointing. "The tower is not a part of the palace, though; we will not be able to see it from here. It is hidden deep in the forest behind a powerful illusion."

Echo wilted a little inside; her legs were already aching, and from where they stood, the entire palace appeared little bigger than the faerie houses she'd constructed from grass and twigs as a child. And that was just to the tower itself. Who knew how many more obstacles might lie in their way? As if in reaction to these thoughts, her stomach abruptly let out a surly grumble. With a sigh, she dropped to the ground and rummaged in her satchel for an apple. Malilia looked confused until the fruit appeared, then nodded understanding and seated herself beside Echo.

"I don't see a better place ahead to stop and have some lunch," Echo explained.

"Forgive me. I forget the mortal need for food."

Echo frowned around a bite of her apple. She crunched slowly and swallowed. "If I am your daughter, why do you keep calling me a mortal?"

Malilia brushed her skirts out. "It is different for changelings. If you chose to stay in Faerthain, your heritage would eventually resurface."

"I thought changelings were all created out of sticks and

flowers and mud. Are you saying… have there been others like me?"

"A few, though the reasons were different."

"How so?"

"In times past, changelings were sometimes left to assess the strength of the mortal realm."

"Like spies?"

"Yes."

Echo took another bite of her apple, pondering this. The question simmering in her mind suddenly broke through her reluctance. "Malilia… what happened to all those other mortal children? The ones the queen stole?"

Malilia's expression darkened like a door slamming shut. "A few of them we were able to return to their parents before the changelings had withered completely."

"Just a few? What about the rest?"

Malilia plucked a blade of grass and wound it around her finger. "If a mortal has some fae ancestry, they tend to fare rather well here. Some of the kinder fae would adopt them, raise them as one of us. Many of them have made good lives for themselves here. A scant number returned to the mortal world, though of course they are bound not to speak of Faerthain or their true identity."

"What about the babies with no magic, whose changelings had already withered?" Echo pressed. She could tell the topic had been intentionally avoided, and it made her stomach turn.

"They…" Malilia hesitated. "They faded."

"Faded? What do you mean?"

A tear shimmered on the woman's cheek. "They died. Sometimes a fae would take pity on one and care for it until it died. Erithea—she was the kindest of all of us—worked hard to find other mortal homes for these unwanted babies, but... she could not save them all."

Echo froze, staring the faerie down, waiting for more, but it was not forthcoming. "And the ones she couldn't save?"

Malilia's face contorted with incredulous pain. "You will force me to say this?"

"You were part of it, weren't you?" Echo demanded.

"I..."

"Yes, I want to know. I want to know what happened after you ripped a child away from all the love it had, and then Titania decided it wasn't good enough for her. So tell me, Malilia." She drew out the name through gritted teeth.

Malilia drew in a breath and said thickly, "They were abandoned. Left alone in the woods to die."

The apple lodged in Echo's throat. She choked; scrabbling to her hands and knees she coughed until the bite of apple flew from her mouth, and then suddenly she was sobbing, her heart shattering. She was falling, plummeting into a well of sorrow.

A gentle touch on her shoulder made Echo pull away in revulsion. "Don't touch me!" she hissed, looking up in time to see the anguish twisting Malilia's features. The fae woman recoiled as though burned, then rose and strode a few steps away, her face turned away, toward the palace.

Echo wept, her arms wrapped around herself as though she could somehow hold the pieces of her heart together. She squeezed her eyes closed, picturing the bereaved mothers whose children would never return. Malilia's agonized expression flashed before her mind's eye, unbidden. Echo tried to blot it out, but she could not. It alternated like that—broken grief, shame and regret—until slowly, her weeping quieted. The skin around her eyes stung as she opened them, her face stiff from tears. Gingerly, she wiped her face with the hem of her dress. Malilia did not turn toward her; she stood rigidly, her shoulders hunched forward.

"How? How could you do it?" Echo demanded, her throat raw.

Malilia continued to stare at the palace. "I could tell you a hundred reasons: my queen commanded it, I coveted her favor, I told myself they were only mortals..." She trailed off. Then she turned and Echo saw tears trailing down the woman's face. "But none of those reasons would matter, because none of them can ever justify what I did. I have tried to make amends in what small ways I could find, but I know that even over a fae's lifetime I would never come close to balancing the scale against me. All I can do is beg the Creator's forgiveness."

Echo pulled herself upright, surprise rippling through her consciousness. "Do the fae know of the Creator?"

"Not many," Malilia replied. "I only learned of him by listening to your father... Gareth, I mean." She plucked aimlessly at her skirt.

Echo frowned, confused. "Dadai? How did you listen to him?"

"I told you, I have been watching you grow up. From a distance, of course, but I couldn't help but come close a time or two when Gareth would read stories." Malilia shook herself. "Come, we still have a long walk ahead of us, and I do not know what obstacles we will find once we reach the tower."

"Obstacles?"

"Queen Titania is thorough in all things," Malilia

explained. "It would not surprise me to find more than just a flight of steps blocking our way."

"Oh." The magnitude of it all overwhelmed her once more with sudden weariness.

"Do not lose heart." Malilia gave her an encouraging smile. "There is yet time to save your sister."

Echo felt as though someone had wound a rope around her ribcage and was slowly tightening it. Emotions she had no name for swam dizzyingly through her mind. With an awkward, jerky motion, she reached out and slipped her hand into Malilia's. The woman started as she looked down at their hands, then up into Echo's face, her eyes searching and confused.

"I'm sorry," Echo whispered. "About earlier, I mean." She chewed on the inside of her cheek, not sure what else to say.

"It was no more than I deserved."

"Dadai says we should treat everyone with kindness, no matter what they deserve. He says it is"—her lips quirked a little at the thought of how he had adopted the phrase she had used as a child—"'vicious disgrateful' to be any less merciful to anyone than the Creator has been to us."

Malilia studied Echo's face for a long moment. She squeezed her fingers tightly before releasing her hand. "Your dadai is a good man."

"The best," Echo agreed.

"Come. If we can reach the forest I know of a place where we can spend the night."

Together, they descended the hill.

THE SUN HAD JUST DIPPED below the horizon by the time they

reached the forest. Malilia plunged into the trees, but Echo hesitated, staring up at the shadowed branches with a quiver of fear. This was not her beloved Faeorn. This misty, ancient wood of tangled undergrowth and creaking, groaning trees would have sent any sane resident of Ennis Rosliath running for a boat, sailing far away from any land which such a forest might inhabit. The spaces between the branches contained a murky, uncanny darkness, and Echo's heart fluttered. She, who had never quailed to enter the Faeorn, found her feet suddenly rooted to the ground in foreboding.

"Echo?" Malilia's face peered out of the gray half-light beneath the canopy. "Is everything all right?"

Echo swallowed with an effort and nodded. Taking a deep breath, she delved into the forest behind Malilia.

The forest did its best to bar their path. Branches snagged at Echo's hair and her clothing. Time and again she had to pause to work a thorny vine out of her skirt so that she could continue.

Bright moonlight cast eerie shadows on the ground, giving the aspect of lurking watchers behind every tree. Somewhere in the distance a chorus of wolves began to sing, their lonely, mournful song sending a chill creeping up Echo's spine.

Her legs ached with weariness, every step became a staggering effort. She struggled to keep her eyes open, but the need for sleep grew more insistent with every passing minute. Her stomach churned, reminding her with a lightheaded queasiness that an apple was not enough sustenance for such a lengthy journey.

At long last, Malilia halted before a dome of woven branches on the edge of a clearing. The moonlight gleamed silver upon the grasses that waved in the open area, painting them with ethereal beauty. It was such a stark contrast to the rest of the forest that Echo's fears fell away, banished by the enchanting scene.

"This is the place I spoke of," Malilia said, and Echo nearly dropped to the ground in weary gratitude. "We can rest here for the night."

They ducked inside the shelter, a single room with ivy and delicate white flowers twined along the branches, both inside and out. Echo entered the hut, her body leaden; she had never been so tired in her life. With a drudging motion she unrolled her blanket, sat down, and retrieved one of Mamai's brown sugar muffins and a little meat pie from her pack. After a moment of thought, she reluctantly offered one to Malilia, but the fae woman shook her head.

"Thank you, but I have my own sustenance."

"Is it true that I could be trapped here if I take something a fae offers me?" Echo asked, a story surfacing in her memory.

"I do not believe so," Malilia replied. "Your fae heritage should protect you from so simple a trick."

Echo frowned. "What, exactly, is my heritage? I've never met a fae before. Well, not a land-fae, I suppose."

"I am a wood-elf," Malilia replied. "As are you."

"Are wood-elves magic?"

"You would probably call it magic." Malilia chuckled. "All the fae have certain capabilities, inherent powers beyond anything a human could do, so I suppose you might call it magic."

Echo's eyelids drooped, but she fought to stay awake. So many questions, but so little time to distill them. It had been... what? Less than three days? since she found out who she was.

"Is my father a wood-elf, too?" she asked sleepily.

Malilia's expression darkened. "He was."

"Was?" Echo's thoughts moved sluggishly in her tired brain; she felt a vague, hollow disappointment. "Did he die?"

"He might as well have." Malilia's tone turned bitter. "He was banished."

"Why?"

Malilia looked away, into the far distance beyond the walls of their bower, her narrow face gray and indistinct in the wan, silvery light that managed to penetrate the roof. "It isn't important. You should sleep now. Tomorrow will be difficult. Sleep."

Echo tried to argue, but an enormous yawn interrupted her and she blinked slowly, lowering herself onto her blanket and curling up with her arm under her head as a pillow. As she drifted off into a deep, dreamless sleep, the last thing she heard was the mournful cry of an owl.

THE TOWER

When Echo awoke, there was no gleam of sunshine to greet her, but what sickly rays filtered onto her face were brighter than the moon had been. She carefully rolled up her blanket and retrieved a croissant from her pack, glad that her mother had insisted on packing enough food to last until the summer solstice. Munching on the pastry, she stepped outside, wondering where her companion had gone. The forest appeared no less forbidding and ominous in the daylight than it had been in the darkness —there was no hint of friendliness or welcome here. Where was Malilia? Echo shivered and tried humming to herself, the music thin and wavering even in her own ears, but it was little use. The burgeoning fear that she had been abandoned coiled itself around her thoughts, strangling her voice until the tune squeaked to an abrupt end, leaving her to brave the dead, empty silence of the wood alone.

She was about to dive back into the flowered dome and concoct some sort of desperate plan when she caught the rhythmic creak of leather on wood. Turning to the sound, she spotted Malilia returning, a bucket of water swinging from one hand.

"I thought you might need this." The faerie smiled. "I drew it from the river, so it should be safe for you to drink."

Relief in the form of a gentle warmth flooded her face as she smiled back and gratefully dipped her flask in the cold water. After a deep draught, she refilled the skin and splashed some of the excess on her face, washing away the film of sweat and grime on her skin. It only made the rest of her body feel dirtier by comparison, but it was refreshing nonetheless.

"Do you have all your belongings?" Malilia asked, stowing the bucket inside the door.

"I'm ready," Echo replied stolidly, strapping her waterskin to her pack.

"Good. The tower stands near the center of the forest. Queen Titania has surrounded it with a powerful illusion, so we must draw very near before it will be visible to us."

"Are you certain you can find it at all?"

Malilia smiled grimly. "I have attended the princess during her isolation; I have searched it out many times before."

"Are there any soldiers?" Echo asked, thinking nervously of the grim-faced guards they had seen at the bridge.

"Not when I was there before," Malilia said. "However, since the guards will have reported the crossing at our border, it is possible that Titania will have taken precautions. I suggest we proceed quickly and cautiously."

When Echo had nodded her assent, the fae woman gestured with one hand and led her onward. With a wary upward glance, Echo followed.

Before long, she was panting, sweat trickling uncomfortably down her back. She irritably brushed long strands of hair away from her damp face and wished she had something to tie it back with. In spite of the deep shade, summer's heat radiated through the air. It didn't help, Echo thought, that they couldn't go more than a few paces without clambering over knobby roots or sliding down rocky escarpments into shallow gullies. Malilia glided forward ahead of her, unhindered by the rough terrain, but Echo kept needing to pause just to catch her breath. She hoped that whatever obstacles lay ahead did not involve anything too dangerous. In Dadai's books, the heroes always had to prove themselves worthy by scaling a hill made of glass or battling a dragon. Echo didn't think she would be very good at anything like that. But she did have Malilia to guide her, and that thought, at least, was comforting.

A sudden tinkling laughter filled the air, so faint it barely registered as real. However, Malilia froze so suddenly that Echo nearly crashed into the wood-elf's back.

"What is it?" Echo asked, once she had regained her balance.

"Hssst." Malilia raised a hand as it sounded again. "Do you hear that?"

"The laughing?" Echo used the unexpected halt to pull out her waterskin and take a long drink from it. "Yes. So?"

"We are close. We must proceed with care."

A breeze rustled through the branches, carrying a moment of sweet relief on its back. Echo let her eyes flutter closed, just enjoying the cool dancing of wind across her hot skin. When she opened her eyes again the entire landscape had changed. She let out a startled exclamation that caused Malilia to whirl about, finger to her lips, a frantic expression in her eyes.

"Wha—?" Echo managed to choke out in a hoarse whisper, and then to her horror, Malilia disappeared.

That same high, innocent laughter came again, but though Echo spun and wheeled, she couldn't find its source, or even its direction. At her feet, something rustled in the grass and a mouse burst through the pine needles, squeaking loudly. Echo uttered a screech of terror and leaped for the nearest tree, a tall fir with long, low-hanging branches. She scrambled up the ladder-like limbs on sheer reflex.

Below her, the tiny rodent was racing back and forth in a strange frenzy, alternating between skittering across the forest floor and standing up, staring at her. Echo shuddered. She loved animals as a general rule, but mice terrified her.

More laughter reached her ears. This time tinged with nastiness. Echo gritted her teeth.

"Who's there?" she shouted, wishing her voice sounded braver.

"Who's there?" a mocking echo replied.

The mouse hopped about at the base of the trunk, and Echo squeezed her eyes shut. Where had Malilia gone? She refrained from shouting the elf's name, but only just.

"Whoever you are, this isn't funny!"

More giggling.

Ignoring the glassy laughter and the dreaded mouse, Echo's gaze flashed around frenetically, trying to get her bearings. The tree she had scaled stood on the edge of a large clearing covered in a blanket of pine needles. Here and there, violets bobbed their heads. In the center of this meadow stood a tower, but it was unlike any tower Echo had ever seen or imagined. Instead of being constructed of stone, the tower was an enormous tree. It soared into the sky, dwarfing its ordinary counterparts. And the branches, instead of spreading out on all sides, stretched up and around into the shape of a small house. Thin strands of ivy wound their way up the trunk, though none of them had ascended beyond the halfway point.

"You smell of mortality," a high voice squeaked in her ear, nearly sending Echo toppling from her perch. She swung her head around, but still could not see anything or anyone who might have spoken.

Another voice, this one lower and more sonorous, replied, "And yet, she also smells of the woodlands. Hmm, and the fae."

"What is it?" the first voice asked.

"It could be human, but that doesn't seem quite right."

"I am human," Echo insisted, pulling herself up haughtily and forgetting that it wasn't precisely true.

"Noooooo," the piping voice replied, drawing out the word. "Definitely not human. But then why does it smell like one?"

"Wood-elf," the second voice announced. "Just like the other one."

Frustration roiled in Echo's chest. She tried to stomp her foot, out of pure habit, but perched as she was, she only succeeded in swinging her leg angrily. "You are both the rudest fae I've ever met!"

A chorus of giggling laughter came in response to this pronouncement.

"It can't have met many fae," the lower voice chuckled.

"We aren't rude!" the trilling voice proclaimed, its voice tinny with indignation.

"Talking about someone where they can hear you but not see you is rude!" Echo shouted.

"Oh! If that's all…" A sparkle of light and color flashed in the air next to the tree and then a creature appeared so suddenly, Echo nearly tumbled backward—again—off her branch.

It was a dragon! But not like any dragon she had ever read about. This creature bore little resemblance to the massive, scaly beasts in her father's books. Barely bigger than the large tom-cat that patrolled their barn, the dragon had delicate features and translucent wings that glistened as they flapped, keeping it aloft. Its scales were a burnt-orange, bounded and ridged with flecks of deep crimson. The creature alighted on the end of her branch, its tail coiling around the limb. It stared at her with bright, amber eyes, then nuzzled its nose around into its flank, scratching at some itch and revealing more of the deep red color on the underside of its scales. Echo felt a sudden compulsion to run her hand over those scales to feel if they were as soft as they appeared.

"A dragon," she breathed.

The little creature preened, its long snout dipping down modestly.

"Drayeth!" The second voice sounded irritated.

"She said we were being rude," Drayeth said.

"We are not to show ourselves to mortals."

"She's not a mortal, Nevyk, you said so yourself."

"There is something strange about her. A smell that is not quite right."

"I know!" Drayeth hopped up and down on his tail, bouncing the tree branch slightly. "Aren't you curious?"

There was another flash of light, this one directly in front of Echo's face, as a slightly larger dragon slowly materialized. This one's scales glittered a deep, midnight blue, with watery edges that ruffled and flared like the fur of a cat who isn't quite sure whether or not he is facing an enemy.

"Of course I'm curious," Nevyk snapped, his amber eyes gleaming as he stared into Echo's face. His nostrils flared. "Wood-elf. Definitely!"

Drayeth hopped some more. "Why did it say it was a human?"

Nevyk's gaze sharpened. "Well?"

"Are you asking me, now?" Echo frowned. The conversation had made her grouchy.

"Well?" Nevyk asked again.

"I don't see why I should tell you." Echo looked away, but her indignation faded as the tower came back into her view and her mind began to race. Dragons. Dragons were supposed to be powerful creatures, or at least, they were in all of her father's stories. True, these were tiny dragons, but Malilia had hinted that more powerful fae creatures might still smell the mortality on her, and these had certainly done so. They could make themselves invisible, and perhaps they were the ones who had made Malilia disappear. In any case, perhaps she could persuade them to help her, if she were clever enough.

"You are a puzzle, and we love puzzles," Drayeth said, as though that should be all the motivation she needed.

"We-ell." Echo paused. "Puzzles shouldn't be easy to solve, should they?"

Both dragons blinked at her. Drayeth uncoiled his tail from the branch and pumped his wings, hovering in the air.

"No!" he exclaimed delightedly. "They shouldn't."

"Tell you what," Echo said. "We can play a game. For every question of mine that you answer, I'll answer one of yours."

Nevyk narrowed his eyes in warning, but Drayeth was already nodding, his serpentine body flowing through the air in a figure eight.

"What are you?" Drayeth blurted.

"Drayeth!" Nevyk spouted a burst of annoyed flame, but it was too late.

"I am a wood-elf." Echo grinned triumphantly. "Now it's my turn." She nodded at the strange tower. "Is that where Princess Jana is being held?"

Drayeth landed solemnly on the branch once more and shot a wary glance at Nevyk.

Nevyk growled at him. "You made the bargain, witless thing."

Drayeth's body drooped. "Yes," he said. "Princess Jana is in the tree house."

Nevyk snapped at the air in front of her face. "What business do you have with our princess, wood-elf?"

"She is my sister," Echo declared boldly. "I've come to rescue her."

"Nonsense," Nevyk replied. "Princess Jana has no sister. Everyone knows that."

"She is my sister, not by blood, but by fortune," Echo said. "And if she does not leave Faerthain before spring's end, she will die."

"What?" Drayeth wobbled on his perch, his eyes wide.

"It's my turn to ask a question," Echo reminded him, and paused, thinking of how best to use the dragons' fascination while it lasted. "How do I get into the tower?"

Drayeth hissed through his teeth and shot a look at Nevyk, who was clearly the older of the two. "You must perform a task set by the guardians to prove your worthiness to stand before the Summer Princess."

"Who are the guardians?" Echo asked.

"My turn," Drayeth snarled, his good humor dissipating. "Why do you smell like a human?"

Echo paused, wondering if she should tell him. But a bargain was a bargain, and she did not see what harm it could do. "I was raised by them," she said. "I've lived in the mortal realm my entire life. Now, my question."

"It is not human, but it may as well be," Drayeth said, drawing his lips back in a sinister grin and revealing a mouth full of tiny daggers. "We are the guardians, faeling. And now our game is done."

A shiver snaked its way up Echo's spine.

15

A DEAL IS STRUCK

"You wish an audience with Her Highness, the Summer Princess?" Nevyk asked.

Echo nodded mutely.

The two dragons shimmered and disappeared. She could still hear their voices, but now they were speaking in a strange, growling language she'd never heard. From her perch on the tree branch she glanced about nervously, wondering again where Malilia had gone.

A moment later, the two dragons reappeared.

"We have decided upon your task," Nevyk said. "You must travel to the center of the forest and bring back a portion of the Everflame."

Echo gnawed on the inside of her cheek. She did not want to appear helpless, but she also did not want to waste the little time she had wandering about aimlessly.

"I have spent my life in the mortal realm," she said, trampling her pride. "I do not know what the Everflame is, and my guide appears to have abandoned me."

"Your guide?" Drayeth asked. "Oh, the other wood-elf? She is still here."

"Where?"

Drayeth swooped to the ground and caught something up in his talons, which he deposited on the branch. Echo stifled her shriek as the tiny brown mouse drew itself up on its hind legs and squeaked vehemently at the dragon.

"Malilia?" Echo gazed at the tiny creature, who nodded slowly and definitely. If a mouse could roll its eyes, this one would have. "I... what?" Echo stared at the dragons in horror. "What did you do to her?"

"It will wear off." Nevyk gave a casual flick of his tail. "Eventually."

"How eventually?"

"A few days at the most."

Echo reached out her hand and allowed the tiny creature to step into her palm, shuddering at the sensation of tiny claws on her skin. Carefully, she slid down from the tree and gently lowered Malilia to the ground before rising to glare at the dragons.

"Since you have deprived me of my guide, the least you could do is tell me what this 'Everflame' is."

"What kind of guardians would we be," Nevyk asked, "if we made it easy? Do not return without the Everflame!" He shimmered and disappeared from sight, his laughter sounding cold and distant.

Drayeth sidled up to her, landing heavily on her shoulder. She winced as his talons pressed into her flesh. He lowered his snout to her ear and she flinched away from its heat, then paused as she heard him whisper, "You say Princess Jana is in danger? What proof do you have?"

"She is a selkie," Echo replied. "She needs to get to the ocean and transform before her thirteenth birthday. I have her skin with me in my pack as proof."

Drayeth paused and seemed to consider this. Then he whispered into her ear once more, "Follow the path of obsidian shards. The Everflame dwells in a lantern guarded by Ritioghra, the ruler of the Winter Fae. He is a shapeshifter, but most often appears as a tiger."

"How am I supposed to steal something from a tiger?"

"Do you have any salt or cold iron?"

"No."

Drayeth gave a little shrug. "Then I do not know. But I wish you well, for my princess' sake."

"If you cared for her at all, you'd help me," Echo growled.

"I just did. To do more would bring the wrath of the queen upon my head." Drayeth pushed off her shoulder, his sudden weight shift making Echo stagger slightly, before he disappeared, too.

Echo slumped to the ground. The mouse scampered up to her knee and Echo suppressed a revolted twitch as it placed a tiny paw on her leg. She glanced up at the tower, thinking about one of the stories in her father's book. A pale face ringed with hair the color of sunset peered through the window. Echo's heart leapt at this glimpse of her sister.

"I don't suppose it would be a good idea for me to skip searching for this Everflame and just climb the tower?"

Mouse-Malilia squeaked in a way that sounded alarmed.

"I didn't think so." She looked down at the tiny creature. "I hope whatever they did to you isn't permanent. Will you go with me to find this Everflame?"

The mouse nodded its tiny head.

"Very well then, hang on." Reluctantly, Echo scooped the creature up and placed it on top of her pack just below her shoulder, trying not to think of how close that was to her hair. She craned her neck and peered down at the mouse. "Any idea which direction this Ritioghra's lair might be?"

The mouse stared at her solemnly and Echo heaved a sigh. "Right. From the way you're looking at me, I'm guessing that if you were yourself you'd be telling me about how dangerous this individual is and that we should stay away from him."

Malilia nodded.

"Well, that's not an option. Drayeth said to follow the path of obsidian shards, which sounds delightful." Echo was not prone to sarcasm, but frustration and despair were manifesting thoughts she would normally keep to herself. She began to pace around the tower, her eyes scanning the ground for any hint of a path leading into the forest. For a moment, she wondered why she was bothering. What had seemed like such a simple undertaking amidst the reassuring security of home and the love it contained had suddenly become a harrowing quest, like in one of her father's stories.

"But I'm not a heroine," Echo muttered. "I'm just… me." A stray thought flickered through her mind, winding tendrils of a terrible idea into her thoughts. Nobody would blame her for turning back now. Far from home, in a strange and hostile kingdom, charged with an impossible task, if she turned around and marched home, nobody would think the less of her. Nobody would even know she had given up. For she had tried. She had come this far. But surely nobody expected her to endanger her own life for a girl she had never met? The thoughts swirled around her, poisonous whispers carried by a gentle breeze that soothed her and murmured that she had done enough, come far enough, that to go on was ridiculous and impossible.

Echo squeezed her eyes tightly shut. "I would know," she whispered. "I would blame me." She conjured up a vision of her parents in her mind's eye, their faces so dear to her it made her heart ache. She missed them fiercely. She remembered the sorrow in their eyes as they had spoken of Jana and she knew she could not turn back. Their love for her buoyed her up in this ocean of despair.

When she opened her eyes, Echo found herself staring down a dark opening in the trees that looked like a tunnel straight into midnight, though all around her the sun still shone brilliantly. The floor of the path glittered with sharp, black stones.

"Shards of obsidian," Echo breathed.

She stepped forward onto the path and immediately winced in pain. Echo was used to going about without shoes, and the soles of her feet were toughened by years of wear. But however carefully she stepped, the stones dug into the soft places between her toes and the fragile skin over the arches of her feet. Every point and ridge seemed designed to drive her off the path. But she didn't dare deviate from the road; in her father's stories, the worst fates always befell those who ignored instruction.

Around her, the forest grew darker and darker until she could barely see even the silhouettes of the trees. She only knew she kept to the correct path by the sharp stones underfoot.

Pausing, Echo knelt carefully and tugged her flint and steel from her pack. Setting the lantern on the ground, she struck the two stones together. They did not produce even the smallest spark. Again and again she tried, but her efforts proved to be in vain, for no amount of careful striking nor begging could convince the wick of the lantern to catch. Finally, she conceded defeat and resumed her trek through the oppressive darkness.

How long she walked, she could not tell. All she knew was the cutting, stabbing pain and the increasing effort of will required to continue moving forward. Her legs began to shake with weariness, and the soles of her feet felt shredded. She limped doggedly on. All at once, the ground shifted beneath her feet, and she stepped down hard on a particularly sharp rock that sliced through the already tattered skin of her foot and sent a shot of agony up through her body. She cried out and stumbled, falling painfully forward. With a whimper, she gingerly pushed herself into a sitting position. In the abject darkness, she could not inspect her own wounds, but she could feel a warm stickiness on her hands and knees and knew she was bleeding.

"What am I doing here?" she cried quietly. "I should have known better than to trust a dragon. This horrible path probably just goes on forever and doesn't lead to the Everflame at all."

Malilia's paw on her shoulder and tickly whiskers on her neck made her shiver.

"It's kind of nice that I can't see you," Echo admitted. "I can pretend you're something other than a mouse."

Malilia squeaked.

"I don't know why they scare me," Echo mumbled, as though the wood-elf had asked. "They just do. Not even spiders bother me the way mice do." She paused, a thought suddenly occurring to her. "Do you know of this Everflame?

I think you can understand me, right? Squeak once for yes and twice for no."

Squeak.

"Am I going the right way?"

Squeak.

"That's encouraging. Any idea how much farther... ugh, I need yes or no questions... well... am I getting close?"

A pause.

Squeak.

"Was that a maybe?" Echo tried to laugh. She started to rise but lancing darts of fiery pain drove her back to her knees. "I can't continue like this," she panted. She pulled her pack open and rummaged about inside until her fingers closed over the handle of her knife. Working slowly and carefully so as not to cut herself, she sliced several strips of fabric from the bottom of her skirt, then bound the strips clumsily.

"You wouldn't think I'd need my eyes for any of that," she said, standing up and testing out her makeshift footwear. The cloth could not, of course, compare with real shoes, but it did offer some scant protection. Gingerly, she limped forward, her eyes straining in the blackness for the tiniest hint of light.

Nothing.

She walked on and on, her pace agonizingly slow, her arms outstretched blindly. The path appeared to be blessedly free of other obstacles—thus far she had not run into any low-hanging branches or even a spiderweb. Perhaps spiders did not like this kind of pure darkness, or perhaps the road was a faerie path between realms and not a place where spiders made their homes. The farther she went, the more she began to believe this theory, for the darkness was too consuming to be natural, and the air itself seemed to be holding its breath. All was still. Even when she paused, no hint of breeze nor chirp of bird reached her. The only realities were the swallowing dark, the pain in her feet, and the occasional prick of Malilia's claws on her shoulder.

16

THE PATH OF OBSIDIAN SHARDS

*E*cho dribbled the last few precious drops of water onto her parched tongue before stowing the empty skin. She still had plenty of food, thanks to Mamai's over-enthusiastic packing, but water would soon become a concern. She had no idea how long she had traveled the path of obsidian shards; time did not exist in this place. The cloths around her feet had grown stiff with sweat and blood. Every step was excruciating. The only hint of progress was the steadily rising temperature. The air hung heavy with humidity and the rocks beneath her feet had grown warm.

Then, so faint that she thought she was imagining it, a glimmer of color appeared in the cheerless world she inhabited. Heart racing, she pressed forward, one painful step at a time, her feet screaming wordlessly while the muscles in her legs begged for relief. She wanted to run, to throw herself at that fragment of color, her heart overjoyed at the reminder that beauty and light still existed, but the cruel stones prevented anything faster than an urgent stumble.

The light grew steadily until she reached its source: an

enormous, black lantern decorated with ornate scrollwork. Inside the glass flickered an intense, brilliantly blue flame.

Echo stared at it, enthralled. The cobalt light seemed to expand, filling her vision until the wood, the darkness, and even the pain she had felt were banished from her mind, quickly followed by every thought that had once dwelt there. There was nothing, had never been anything, but this light, nothing but this perfect, all-consuming fire. Its light was everything. No other beauty could exist in a world where the Everflame blazed.

She stood before it, swaying with the dancing refractions it cast on the ground. All thoughts of her quest had fled. She would gladly stay here for eons, simply studying that mesmerizing cerulean...

A sharp pain in her shoulder pierced the trance. Tearing her gaze away from the lantern, she glared down at the tiny mouse.

"Did you just bite me?"

The mouse regarded her accusingly.

"I..." Echo trailed off, her mind clearing. "Oh." She blew out a breath, feeling a tremble beginning in her knees. How long might she have stayed there? "I suppose I should say thank you then." She glanced around, careful not to stare directly into the lantern again, and found a yawning cave beyond it. She could not see further than the entrance, but it gave her a shivery feeling, and she had no desire to get any closer to the gaping maw. "I don't see the guardian anywhere," she whispered to Malilia. With deft fingers she unhooked her own lantern and held it up, wondering how she could transfer some of the blue flame without burning herself.

She took a step forward and found that the ground

around the lamp post was blessedly smooth, cool, and—most importantly—free of sharp edges. She breathed a sigh of relief and resisted the urge to inspect her poor, mangled feet. The thought of stepping back onto that tortuous path and following it back to the tower was more than she could bear, so instead she focused on the task at hand.

"You dare steal from the King of the Winter Court?" The voice reverberated through the air, its sheer, palpable power pushing Echo to her knees. The lantern dropped from her nerveless hand and clattered on the ground.

Echo bowed her head respectfully, racking her memory for every snatch of folk-tale she had ever heard about the Winter Fae or the Dark Host. "Forgive me, my lord," she whispered. "I did not intend to steal from you. I merely seek to save the life of my sister."

She heard soft footfalls approach across the sable ground but she did not dare raise her eyes, not even when she felt the touch of hot breath on the back of her head.

"You smell of truth." The voice sounded puzzled. "Rise, seeker."

Echo stood, wincing at the pain in her feet. But that thought fled with the rest as she came face to face with the largest tiger she had ever seen.

Upon reflection, it was the only tiger she had ever seen. But she was reasonably certain that, should she ever see another, it would be quite different from the monstrous beast that confronted her now.

Her eyes were even with his shoulders, and he stared down at her from his impressive height, his long whiskers twitching inches above her face. His fur was utterly black, the color of coal. Instead of stripes, Ritioghra's—for it could only be Ritioghra—body was covered in swirls and whorls of gleaming blue, the same color as the Everflame. His eyes gleamed like two massive stars of an identical shade, and he gazed down at her with an expression of ferocious curiosity. He was utterly terrifying and utterly beautiful.

Terror coursed through her veins like ice, but the light of intelligence in his eyes gave her courage. "For-forgive me, my lord." Echo gave a wobbly curtsy.

The tiger stretched with a lazy nonchalance. Every line of his long body rippled with power and strength, like the unstoppable force of a river about to burst its banks.

"Tell me of this sister whose life you seek to save. But have a care; I will know if your words are untrue." His voice, though gentle, pounded over her like the rhythm of the ocean waves that hurled themselves against the cliff beneath her house.

Echo's mouth went dry. His unexpected civility disarmed her. "I... er... haven't met her," she confessed. "I was left in her cradle as an infant."

"A changeling?" the Winter King echoed with surprise. "That would explain your odd aroma."

Echo grimaced. Did all the fae have highly sensitive noses? It wasn't a trait she'd ever noticed in herself, and she wasn't sure she wanted to experience that kind of acute sense of smell.

"Yes," was all she said, however. "My sister is a selkie. She has been imprisoned by the fae." That much was true, at least, if only from her own point of view. "If she doesn't return to the sea before the first day of summer, she will die."

The tiger's whiskers twitched. "And what do you care if she does?"

The question was so unexpected that Echo wasn't sure she even understood it. "Um... what?"

"You call this girl your sister, but what bonds of family can tie you to someone you have never met?"

"I..." She paused. "My parents grieve her loss. I... I hope that returning her to them will ease their sorrow."

"A magnanimous gesture, indeed." The tiger purred. Then he lowered his face to regard her directly. "But what if her return to her rightful place leaves you without one?"

A shudder worked its way through Echo's body as the tiger spoke the words she had dared not think. What if he was right? What if the return of the true daughter, the one who shared her father's blood and her mother's heritage, pushed Echo to the edges of their hearts? Oh, they would claim to love her still, having raised her, but Jana was the daughter they had lost. Only she could heal the hole in their hearts. Echo tried to imagine sharing her loft with a stranger, knowing that other girl would always hold the first, and perhaps only, portion of their parents' love. Her jaw clenched of its own accord.

"It is a noble thing you attempt," Ritioghra said, a deep, rumbling purr surrounding his words. "But perhaps it would be best if you failed."

To her horror, Echo felt her head begin to nod. She froze. What had he done to her? His velvet words had corrupted her thoughts like venom.

"No!" she burst out. "My parents..." She faltered.

"Your parents do not care about you. If they did, why would they send you alone into the dangerous realm of the fae?"

"They..." Echo raised her chin, finding strength in the truth. "They did not send me alone. My father tried to come, but he is mortal and could not pass through the gate. I slipped away while he slept." She felt Malilia's claws on her back as the mouse slipped down her back to the ground. She could only guess at the wood-elf's designs, but she assumed it would be best to keep the Winter King's attention away from the tiny creature.

Ritioghra tossed his great head and circled her, his enormous paws perfectly stealthy on the ground. His tail flicked across her shoulder blades, the solid weight of it making her stagger.

"Tell me, seeker: why does your quest bring you to the doorstep of my domain? What threatens your sister's life that the Everflame can save her? My flame is powerful, but healing is not its usual application. If this girl needs to get to the sea, its light will not transport you there."

Echo bit her tongue. She did not know much about the fae courts; as of a few days ago, she had not believed they even existed. But she had heard the stories, and most of what she had encountered thus far suggested to her that those stories held some truth, in which case it was safe to assume that the Winter King was not on friendly terms with the Summer royals. Out of the corner of her eye, she saw the mouse scampering up the lantern's pole.

"I don't need the Everflame to heal her." Echo chose her words carefully. "I need it to reach her."

The tiger cocked his head, lowering himself into a crouch. "Explain."

"My sister is sick, it is true. But she is also a prisoner. Her guards promised to let me see her in exchange for a bit of the Everflame."

The tiger prowled about, the blue swirls covering his body pulsing with light, as though they were connected to the very beat of his heart.

He whirled on her and Echo leaped back. She lost her

balance and fell, catching herself painfully on her elbows. The Winter King loomed over her, his lips pulled back in a snarl.

"You are trying to deceive me!" he roared.

"I have told you no lies," Echo said, trying to keep her voice steady.

The tiger withdrew with a low growl and Echo pulled herself up into a wary crouch, watching him pace.

"Perhaps, perhaps, but you are keeping something back," the Winter King snarled. He paused and turned his face away from her, raising a paw and cleaning it roughly with his tongue. "The stories about me are not true," he said, his voice returning to its smooth, sonorous timbre. "Your quest is a noble one, and you have a noble heart. I am inclined to give you a portion of my Everflame. However, I have a final question."

Echo tensed. Malilia had ascended to the lantern and was reaching inside, awkwardly manipulating a white object toward the fire. She frowned, then recognized the paper spill from her pack.

The Winter King glanced at her. "What is your sister's name?"

Echo barely heard the question. Malilia had angled the spill down and was lowering it into the flame.

"Jana," Echo answered without thinking.

A thunderous roar echoed through the darkness, shaking the ground. In the midst of the deafening sound of rage, Echo realized her mistake. She groped for her own lantern even as the spill in Malilia's paws curled, blackened, and lit.

She caught up the handle of her lantern and clipped it to her pack even as she lurched forward, reaching for Malilia.

"The Summer Queen's daughter?" Ritioghra roared again and pounced toward her.

The mouse leaped from her perch, causing the light to swing madly about the darkened space as the Winter King's enormous frame landed next to Echo, his hot breath wafting across her face.

"You did not tell me you came on an errand from the Summer Queen." His voice rumbled with menace. "No subject of the Summer Court is welcome here, and any who foolishly tread upon my threshold may never leave this place."

"I am no subject of the Summer Court," Echo said, her voice rising in fear. "I have told you the truth."

"You are in league with my enemies and have brought one here to my domain! You sought to steal from me all the while. You will not have any part of the Everflame!"

Echo scooped Malilia up off the ground. With a cry, she fled the circle of blue light, dashing recklessly into the darkness once more. The tiger's enormous paw swept out, his claws catching her pack and raking the tender skin of her back, throwing her off balance. Echo screamed and fell, one hand curled in toward her body to protect Malilia. She landed hard on her back, her breath leaving her chest in a terrible gasp. She lay there for a moment, her mouth opening and closing as she fought to refill her lungs. The gouges on her back throbbed with fiery intensity, her heart pumping blood out through the deep scratches onto the unyielding ground. After what felt like hours, but was probably only a few seconds, she regained some of her breath. Rolling painfully onto her stomach, she pulled herself forward on her elbows, away from the Winter King's wrath. At any moment she expected to feel his teeth clenching down on her skin, but the seconds passed, her breath coming in ragged, tearing inhalations as she dragged herself along with agonizing slowness, and no retribution came. Behind her, she could hear the tiger's furious roars, but he did not pursue them.

She continued to feel her way back through the darkness. Every movement brought a new wave of agony sluicing through her body, but Echo gritted her teeth against the pain, terrified of making any sound that might lead the Winter King after her. As time passed, she felt the cuts on her back begin to stiffen with dried blood, and their agony subsided into a throbbing ache. She had no idea whether she was even going in the right direction, but there was nothing to do but persist and hope that she would not be lost forever in this dark place between the realms.

Slowly, the blackness receded, replaced by a pale, silver glow of a forest. Her fingers crunched into the detritus of a forest floor, sending up a rich, earthy aroma, and Echo flopped down, burying her face in the blessedly familiar softness.

Memory pricked her thoughts and she sat up in a rush, wincing as the sudden movement tore open some of her cuts.

"Malilia?"

The little mouse was nowhere to be seen. Echo whirled, panic rising until a hand settled gently on her shoulder.

"I am here."

She looked up into the face of the wood-elf relieved to see her not only present, but restored to her true form.

"You were doing well," Malilia murmured. "I should not have interfered."

"I thought you had..." Echo shook her head. "Thank you

for trying. I saw what you did. I'm sorry... I messed every-thing up. I should have known better than to reveal Jana's name to him..."

"No, I am sorry. I believe the Winter King would have granted you what you sought had I not been there."

A flash of white on the ground nearby caught Echo's eyes. Her heart leapt at the sight. From the paper spill rose a trickle of smoke! She caught it up, hope blossoming in her chest as she noted the gleam of an ember, but even as she scrambled for her lantern, the thin gray wisp sputtered, then dissipated entirely, leaving nothing but char and ash to prove it had ever been.

The flame had died.

"What do I do now?" Echo whispered.

17

RIDDLES AND RESOLVE

The forest sang with life as Echo leaned her cheek on her knees and dropped the charred bit of paper, feeling hollow and heartsick. They could not go back; she knew they would never escape Ritioghra a second time. Yet the dragons would never admit her without the Everflame, either. Feeling lost, she idly surveyed their surroundings, but something seemed wrong, or rather, right.

"Wait... where are we? This looks like the Faeorn, but... how is that possible?"

"It is the Faeorn," Malilia confirmed. "We fled the Winter King without taking care which path we took and have come back out in the mortal realm."

"I'm home?"

The weight of that truth settled in the pit of her stomach. She could just go back. Traitorously, her head turned in the direction of the little cottage out on the peninsula, the snug haven over the crashing ocean.

Home. By the angle of the light coming through the trees, Mamai would be starting supper soon, and Dadai would be finishing up at the docks. Were they worried for her? Could they sense she had returned to the mortal realm where she belonged? The forest, at least, seemed to embrace her with the warmth of a long-lost friend.

Malilia's sharp intake of breath pulled Echo from her thoughts and she turned to see what new danger approached. But Malilia's eyes were fixed on Echo, an expression of horror flooding her features.

"You're bleeding!" Malilia cried out, rushing forward as if afraid that Echo might collapse.

At her words, Echo recalled the slice of the tiger's claws across her back, and she twisted, craning her neck in an attempt to see how badly she had been slashed. But the motion wrenched the skin around the wounds, and when the haze of pain had cleared, she abruptly found herself sitting in a pile of pine needles with no memory of how she had gotten there. Malilia's thin brown hands were on her shoulders.

"Stay still!" the wood-elf ordered.

Echo did not argue. Her head spun and the world seemed to fade in and out of focus with the pulse of her heartbeat. Malilia knelt behind her. Echo heard the trickle of water and then gasped as the elf pressed something cool and damp against her wounds.

"We'll have to wrap the bandage around you," Malilia told her.

Numbly, Echo sat beneath Malilia's gentle ministrations. When the woman had tended to her back, she moved on to Echo's feet, loosing the makeshift bandages that were now caked with blood and dirt. The sight of her flayed skin brought the world to a grinding halt. Blackness darker than the Winter King's path flooded her vision like the rising tide. The next thing she knew, she was drowning. Echo bolted upright, choking and coughing, and glared accusingly at a startled Malilia.

"I only passed out; there's no need to drown me!" she snapped.

"I only splashed you a little!" Malilia replied. "I got worried when you wouldn't waken!"

Echo frowned. It only felt as though she'd been out for a few seconds, but a glance at her feet showed they had been cleaned and properly bandaged. Experimentally, she pushed herself up off the ground and stood, swaying slightly. Her body ached and her feet throbbed, but the pain had diminished somewhat.

"I also brewed some willow bark tea for the pain." Malilia nodded to a small cook-fire over which she had contrived to hang a boiling pot of water.

"Thank you," Echo said. She seated herself by the fire, every part of her stiff and sore. Her stomach rumbled. The sun had dipped lower in the sky, but this close to summer, Echo knew that they would have light for a few more hours. She pulled out some dried meat and a biscuit and devoured them both. Then she sipped Malilia's tea, slowly, so as not to burn her tongue. The warm liquid trickled down her throat pleasantly, pushing back the chill that had taken up residence during her talk with the Winter King and soothing the aches in her body. They were mournfully silent as the fire began to burn down, its utility spent.

"What do we do now?" Echo mumbled. "Do you think I can persuade those dragons to let me speak with Jana even if I don't bring the Everflame?"

"No," Malilia sighed resignedly. "You made a bargain—a sacred pact, to the dragon-fae. They will kill you before they let you break the agreement. You will not be able to sneak past them, either. They may be small, but they are powerful. Turning me into a mouse was a fairly benign—if quite uncomfortable—display of their strength."

"Well, I can't face Ritioghra again!" Echo exclaimed in panic.

"No." Malilia grimaced. "He would be waiting for you. Had I been capable of speech, I would have told you of his feud with Titania and Oberon. He wished to marry Jana, thereby securing an alliance between the Summer and Winter courts. They have refused his proposals, mostly because they wish to keep the princess's illness a secret."

"I should not have said her name." Echo sucked on her lip, cupping the earthenware mug in both hands just below her nose. She glanced down at it in surprise. "Where did this come from?"

Malilia lowered her eyes. "I fashioned it with glamour."

Echo twisted it about, studying it. "It is... simpler than I would have expected."

"The simpler the object, the less energy it requires. You needed function, not form."

"Thank you." She took another slow sip, then rose painfully to her feet, grimacing. Hopelessness flooded through her thoughts in a red haze. "I just... I just want to go home," she admitted in a small voice. In her heart, she had already given up the quest, but now she said the words aloud. "I can't do this. I thought I could, but..." She shook her head, choking on a mixture of fear and shame. "I'm not a hero. I wanted to be brave, and strong, like in Dadai's stories... but I'm not. Jana has royal parents and powerful dragons guarding her. She doesn't need me. I just want to go home."

Malilia gave a slow nod. "I understand." Her voice

sounded soft. "You have already done more than anyone would have asked."

Echo hesitated, a war erupting within her emotions. She took a step in the direction she knew her home lay. Another step. Her heart fractured into a million pieces, but she could not muster the courage to return to that glade, nor to face that terrible tiger.

A whooshing sound filled the air and then a flurry of white filled Echo's vision and she ducked as a large, snowy owl swooped down over her head and landed on Malilia's shoulder. It gave a gentle hoot and plucked at a strand of the wood-elf's hair with its beak.

Echo gazed at the bird, who stared unblinkingly back at her, and she felt a tiny shred of courage ignite deep within herself.

"Hello again." Echo smiled as she noted the peculiar golden mark on the owl's wing.

"You've met?" Malilia looked surprised.

Echo nodded and the owl made a gentle warbling sound. Malilia smiled.

"You remember that in the future," she chided, stroking the downy feathers on the owl's breast.

Echo's fingers itched to touch those soft feathers, and she took a tentative step closer. "The path we took to the Everflame... It can't be the only way to get there. I mean, we clearly left by a different route."

"The Everflame is accessible from all the realms," Malilia replied. "The Winter King has claimed it for over a century now and guards it jealously, but it is not truly part of his domain."

"So it doesn't really belong to him?"

"No." Malilia shook her head. "The Everflame exists in

a... different... place. It is... hard to explain. You were there, you saw the cavernous space—it is uninhabited, and yet it is linked to all the realms."

"A doorway," Echo mused.

"Yes, there are many paths leading to the Everflame. The Winter King is most vigilant over the one we took. He is paranoid that Oberon wishes to steal it." She tapped her chin. "He is not wrong, of course."

"Then there might be a way to get there from here that he wouldn't see?" Echo asked skeptically. The glade in which she had met the Winter King might be dark, but it also lacked anything to hide behind.

"Ritioghra cannot spend all his time prowling around his treasure. He has his Dark Court to rule. My guess is that he has woven some magic to alert him if anyone should approach from the Summer Court—along the obsidian path we followed."

"Do you know where the doorway from this realm might be?"

Malilia shook her head. "The only door I'm familiar with is the one we used to get there from Faerthain."

Echo reached out a finger and gently stroked the owl's downy breast. "I don't suppose you know where the entrance to the Everflame glade might be?"

The bird gave a trilling hoot and thrust itself into the sky, soaring about them in a tight circle, before arrowing away from them through the trees.

Echo and Malilia shared a look full of wonder, then started after the owl. Within a few steps, however, Echo's body mutinied against the sudden exertion, and cloudy darkness tunneled her vision once more. She gave a little cry of pain and nearly fell, but Malilia was there, propping her up and helping her along, following their silent-winged guide.

Her arm around the wood-elf's shoulders, Echo stumbled and limped through the familiar landscape of the Faeorn. Through the trees, the sun sank down to the horizon, casting a fiery glow of red and gold between the lengthening shadows. They followed the owl until it at last came to land, perching on a thick branch in a familiar location.

The owl had led them to the huge, ancient trees known as the Guardians. They towered over the darkened schoolhouse and its abandoned yard; down the hill they could see the outskirts of the village, and beyond that, the dark blue of the ocean stretching away to the horizon.

For a moment, Echo stood in blinking confusion. Then she straightened, her weariness falling away.

"Malilia!" she burst out. "The gateway at the bridge—it only opens at certain times, right?"

The wood-elf nodded. "Dawn and twilight, though the door never opens for mortals unless the fae are in the mood to play tricks."

"Do other doors work that way?"

"Some."

A memory tickled at the back of Echo's mind, bringing with it a flood of shame. What if Branna hadn't been teasing her? A blue glow coming from an ancient pair of trees at twilight? Could her story have been true after all?

Echo strode as steadily as she could manage up to the Guardians and peered into the large hollow. She ducked inside and felt about the interior, her hands running over the divots and recesses of its inner surface. Nothing. She peered at the sun, which had fallen to rest on the edge of the earth. Twilight would soon be upon them.

Malilia rested a hand against the tree, her head tilted back, staring up at the massive branches with an expression of awe across her features.

"Will twilight be enough to open the door?" Echo asked. "Or do I need to do more?"

Malilia pursed her lips. "Perhaps you should ask the Guardians themselves."

"Ask the trees?"

"You are a wood-elf, after all."

Echo came slowly to stand beside her mother. "How do I speak with them?"

"You can call to them; you know that we cannot force them to answer."

Echo studied the old sentinel. Despite its age, it stood straight and tall, a warrior keeping watch. She had always loved this tree, often noticing it through the schoolhouse window while the teacher gave her lecture.

"Please." Echo curtsied. "I know you guard a secret way to the Everflame, and I need to pass through it in order to save the life of my sister. Will you help me?"

A breeze rustled through the leafy branches of the ancient oak. Then a tall, thin man stepped out from behind it. Echo gaped, thinking at first that some villager had been hiding there, but then she realized that she had never seen this man before. His skin was the color of weathered drift-wood, and his dark green eyes caught her own and held, and she felt she could read books of knowledge written there, if she only knew the language. Tufts of white hair stuck out from his head and a long, hoary beard strung with wooden beads hung from his chin. Yet, despite his apparent age, his back was straight and he walked without faltering.

"The wind has brought me the tale of your quest." The old

man spoke, and his voice creaked like the sound of great tree trunks bowing before a breeze. "I will not bar your passage, but you must open the door."

"But I don't know how, and twilight is nearly here!" Echo cried.

The old man smiled. "I will ask you three riddles. If you can answer correctly, I will tell you how to open the portal."

Echo raised her eyebrows. She liked riddles; it was something she shared with her father. He had told her many over the years, and she had eventually solved all of them, though none of them had carried such gravity. However, a glance at the sky told her that she had little time to ponder. She gave a tight nod.

The guardian peered at her, a flicker of a smile touching his lips as he began to speak. "You will find it in the caves, though its voice is weak; it has no mouth and yet it speaks. It has no ears with which to hear, yet it will answer, never fear."

A chuckle escaped her mouth. This was one of her favorites, because she felt a bit of ownership for it. "An echo!" she exclaimed.

"Hmmm," the old man hummed. "Correct." He held up two fingers. "Half my life is lived in death; though footless, I dance, and breathe without breath. What am I?"

Echo furrowed her brow. The sun had turned orange and had fallen halfway behind the rim of the world. Half my life is lived in death. What could that mean? And what could breathe without breath? She frowned, growing worried. Her mind raced as the light began to fade.

A wind rattled through the forest, the branches swaying as if to some secret song... almost like... dancing? And in the winter, its limbs would sway, barren... dead?

"A tree," Echo proclaimed with what she hoped was confidence.

The old man narrowed his eyes at her, and Echo held her breath, but then he smirked. "Aha! Perhaps we are being too generous. Let us try something harder, shall we?" He hummed a bit, then his lips stretched back into a cunning grin. "Always abandoned, born without a skin, I shouted once, then ne'er spoke again."

Echo's thoughts immediately turned to her mother and sister. Surely the answer had something to do with selkies? Or perhaps changelings? She herself had been abandoned, and Malilia had revealed to her that many of the mortal children the queen didn't want had also been abandoned to a terrible fate. The word "changeling" was on the tip of her tongue, and yet she hesitated. Always abandoned? She couldn't claim that. Her parents, Mamai and Dadai, they had never abandoned her. Even though they knew she wasn't their own, they had chosen to raise her and love her, never treating her as anything less than their beloved daughter.

Selkies, then? But that didn't seem right either. Nothing in the riddle seemed to apply to her mother, the only selkie she knew.

Echo closed her eyes, shutting out the waning daylight, and mulled over the puzzle, turning it over in her mind and examining it from every angle. What only spoke once? And then only in a shout? An image flashed across her mind of her mother leaving the house at night, long hair streaming behind her in the driving wind and rain, her disappearing form illuminated by streaks of lightning... lightning that streaked across the sky, leaving behind... or perhaps, abandoning...

Echo's eyes flew open.

"Thunder!" she shouted as the last ray of sunlight winked out.

The old man clapped his hands once. "Quite so." He smiled. "Knew you were up to the challenge. Circle the ancient Guardian three times against the clock in the twilight hour, and the door shall open for the clever girl."

The urgency of vanishing time like a sounding horn in her mind, Echo turned to her right and limped as quickly as her wounds would allow around the mighty trunk. By the time she finished the third pass, the old man was gone, but she had little attention for his absence. For there in the hollow of the ancient tree, flickered a familiar, eerie blue light.

Branna had been sincere. Echo's conscience smote her as she realized how hurtful her own response must have been. She would apologize, if she ever returned. But first, the Everflame, and Jana.

Taking a deep breath, Echo ducked her head and plunged down the newly opened path.

18

THE EVERFLAME

*T*he path beneath the Guardians bore no resemblance to the road of obsidian shards she had traversed the day before. Or had it only been hours? Traveling between worlds had demolished her understanding of time. Thankfully, although the new way was riddled with knobs and bumps, there were no sharp edges; in fact, the wooden surface was worn down and polished smooth, like an ancient floor that had known hundreds of years of passing feet.

"It's like... roots?" she whispered to Malilia.

"Well, it is set in a tree," the wood-elf murmured back.

Though darkness was falling on this side of the portal it was not as thick as it had been on the first journey. She could not see much beyond her own outstretched hand, but there was a faint turquoise hue to the air that already seemed to be intensifying. A few steps later, she found herself standing beneath another doorway, this one made of smooth, beautiful branches that had been woven into a pointed arch. Blue flowers twined around the doorframe at this edge of the clearing, and in the center of that open space stood the Everflame. Echo blinked, surprised at how much shorter this journey had been. Then she frowned at the archway. It had no door; what could be the point of such a structure? And why hadn't she seen it the first time?

Peering into the gloaming, Echo saw that the clearing appeared deserted, but Malilia was hanging back.

"Are you coming?" Echo asked.

Malilia shook her head. "My presence will surely alert the Winter King. Besides, I... have someone I need to speak with."

At the thought of Ritioghra, Echo's courage faltered, and the wounds on her back throbbed anew. She did not want to face the Winter King again, yet she did not want to spend another minute in that darkened corridor either. All she wanted at that moment was to be home, home where her greatest trial was mucking Grainne's stall, home where the safety of her mother's arms was always within reach. She wanted to listen to her father tell her Bible stories or teach her how to tie knots. She longed for the Faeorn with its cool, soft ferns, where she could lose herself in a book or climb a tree, and her only worry was to be home in time for dinner.

"You do not have to do this," Malilia said tentatively, as though reading Echo's thoughts. "I can take you home."

"No." Echo shook her head. "Until the sun sets on the first day of summer, there is hope. As long as there is hope, I have to try."

Malilia's eyes softened. "Very well. When you have the Everflame, look for the obsidian road. It will lead you back to Faerthain. I will meet you there."

Echo grimaced at the thought of setting foot back on that terrible path.

"And beware. Recall how the Everflame entrances those who look upon it."

Echo chewed the inside of her cheek and nodded.

"I will see you soon." Malilia seemed tempted to linger, but then she turned, her hands stiff at her sides, and retreated back up the path the way they had come.

Hardly daring to breathe, Echo crept through the doorway, her feet treading lightly on the glassy floor. She happened to glance down and sucked in a stunned breath: instead of her reflection, she was looking into the bottomless depths of a starry night. She bit down a shriek and jerked her chin back up, heart racing. That cosmic vista was fathomlessly, devastatingly beautiful. It was also profoundly unnerving; she hadn't actually seen any hint of the floor. It had looked like she should have plummeted into that vast, eternal expanse. How many mortals could say they had trod upon the very sky? Echo's head spun and she fought the impulse to look again, instead fixing her gaze somewhere near the Everflame, careful not to look directly at its enthralling gleam. Why did everything in this strange realm have to be so perilously alluring?

Her feet padded whisper-soft across the room, bringing her within a few paces of the fire. No sign of the Winter King. Perhaps she could creep past unnoticed. Her spirits lifted as she stepped up to the gleaming, ornate lantern.

A rumbling growl resounded through the glade and Echo froze, her heart trying to bolt from her chest.

"So, the thief returns," the familiar velvet voice purred behind her.

Slowly, achingly slowly, Echo turned to face the Winter

King. His tail was curled around his haunches, its tip just barely twitching. She wondered if he had been waiting for her, or if his comfortable demeanor only made it look like he had been sitting there for hours. Either way, he cut a royal figure.

"I am no thief," Echo replied, her voice emerging in a tremulous warble.

"Nor are you a subject of the Summer Court." He narrowed his eyes at her. "I told you I can smell lies. After you fled, I realized—albeit belatedly—that you had spoken the truth. It is not often that I apologize, or admit that I was in the wrong, as I rarely am." He raised an enormous paw and gave it a few leisurely passes with his tongue, then he put it down and fixed her with a steady gaze. "I say all this so that you may appreciate how momentous an occasion this is to which you are now witness." He stood and stretched lazily, then took two padding steps forward so that he stood so close she could feel his breath on her face.

Terror swelled within her. Those mighty jaws could easily snap her in two. She concentrated on breathing normally and holding her body still, but it was all she could do not to run screaming into the darkness.

Then, slowly and deliberately, Ritioghra bowed his head until his chin nearly touched the floor. "My deepest apologies, my lady. I have doubly wronged you. The Winter King may be many things, but dishonorable is not one of them. I am indebted to you by blood and by judgment, and as such, I will grant you two boons, provided they be in my power. Choose carefully, for if you ask something I cannot grant, the request is still spent."

Echo stared at him in bewilderment. She had no idea how to respond to this, but the weight of power settled upon her like a physical thing. Wildly, her first thought was to ask him to free her sister, but before she opened her mouth she had already discarded the idea. It would be a rash and wasteful wish. He could no more infiltrate Faerthain and steal the princess than she could sprout wings and fly.

"I am honored, Your Majesty." Echo bobbed a stiff curtsy. She chose her next words carefully, mindful of anything that could be construed as a request. "I would appreciate a moment to consider my two requests."

His blue eyes danced with amusement. "Well spoken." He settled himself onto the ground and absently licked his other paw. "So… this sister you seek to save is the Summer Princess. Long have I sought to arrange a marriage between her and myself in an attempt to ally the two fae courts."

"I know."

"You do?"

"I also know that King Oberon and Queen Titania have denied your attempts."

"Yes. And you brought me the answer as to why. I must thank you. That knowledge has provided me with a power I have never held over the Summer Court before."

A shudder of terrible responsibility spiked through Echo at his words, but she shrugged it away. The fae courts and their intrigues were not her concern. They had gone on for centuries before her, and would probably continue for long centuries after.

"I am not a monster," Ritioghra continued, "though the stories always paint me as such. The evil ruler of the Unseelie Court—it is not true. Perhaps my domain seems harsher, and my rule more strict than that of the fair Summer Court, but it is by necessity, not cruelty, that this is so." He rose and prowled restlessly in a large circle before returning to sit next to the glimmering lantern.

"I have decided upon my first request," Echo said.

"Ask."

"I would like a small portion of the Everflame to take with me when I leave this place." She was proud of herself for keeping her voice as steady as she did.

"Ah yes, the thing you came for in the first place. Come closer."

Reluctantly, Echo obeyed, though she had no desire to get within reach of those wickedly sharp claws, even if they were currently sheathed.

"Your request is virtuous and your heart is noble. There are not many who could remain so selfless in the face of the gift I offered. Hold up your lantern."

Echo obeyed. The Winter King raised one paw and a tiny flicker of blue fire, no bigger than that of a candle's, divested itself from the Everflame and drifted over to ignite the wick within Echo's lantern. Echo closed the little door and gave another small curtsy.

"I thank you, Your Majesty."

"I wish you success on your quest, Noble Heart." His voice enveloped her like a warm embrace, the words purring in her ear. "Perhaps I have been hasty in other areas. I could do worse than a bride such as yourself. What would you say to the offer of ruling a kingdom at my side?"

Echo stumbled backwards, horrified. "I would say that I am far too young for marriage!" she squeaked, hoping this would not be too rude of a refusal.

A deep chuckle emanated from the Winter King's throat and Echo's face flamed as she realized that the tiger had not been in earnest. "Ah." He bared sharp teeth below eyes dancing with amusement. "Well, then perhaps I shall ask when you are older. Now, your second request?"

Ruffled by his unexpected teasing, a thousand thoughts and ideas flashed through Echo's mind. To see her parents, just for a moment; to go home; to wake up and find that all of these trials had been nothing more than a strange and terrible nightmare... But no, this quest of hers must be accomplished. And while many obstacles may yet befall her, she could only ask to avoid the one she knew.

"Could you..." she began, her words timid, her tired brain finally overcome by all that she had been through. "I mean... would you please..." She paused, taking a moment to gather herself back together. "I must return to Faerthain. And I'm afraid that if I travel that road again, it will be too much for me, and I will fail, or at least be crippled by the time I arrive, and no good to my sister. Can you bring—or send—me to the clearing where Jana's tower stands, without having to follow the obsidian path?"

Ritioghra gave a startled laugh. "I like you better and better," he exclaimed. "Such wisdom is rare indeed, especially in one so young." He rose. "This boon I will also grant. Farewell, Noble Heart. You are a brightness in a land that is, perhaps, too dark at times. May our fates mingle again soon."

Before Echo could construct a polite way to reply that she hoped exactly the opposite, the tiger gave a rumbling roar and the Everflame flared, swelling until it broke free of its lantern and reached out to enfold her in its embrace. Echo bit back a scream as the icy flames consumed her, chilling her to the bone with their wintry touch. The world glowed with a cobalt hue, pulsing around her with growing intensity until she thought she might shatter like an icicle falling to the ground, but then it receded and the blue light faded. As the world came back into focus, she found herself back in the clearing below the tower, a gentle flurry of snow falling to the ground around her. The delicate flakes landed on her cheeks, icy kisses dissipating as they caught the sunlight. Echo raised her arms to the heat of bright midday, exulting in the return of light and color and warmth.

19

THE SUMMER PRINCESS

*a*s the snowflakes around her melted, disappearing into the sunshine-infused air, Echo heard a familiar giggle. She held up her lantern, its small but valiant flame flickering a deep shade of blue.

"I have returned with what you asked!" she called out loudly. "And I now hold you to our bargain."

The flame-scaled dragon winked into sight, his eyes wide as he approached, peering into the lantern. "You... you..." He abruptly vanished again, leaving Echo staring at the spot where he had been.

A roiling anger coursed over her thoughts. She was exhausted and hungry, she ached all over, her back throbbed where the tiger's claws had slashed her skin, her feet stung as though a thousand fire ants were actively biting her, and she had no idea how long it had been since she had last slept. She spun in a circle, defiantly thrusting the lantern aloft.

"I demand to speak with Princess Jana! I kept my part of the deal and brought back your precious Everflame; now keep your side of it or I will call for the queen herself to judge between us! Perhaps she won't like knowing that anyone can get past her guards with the right sort of bargain!" Echo stamped her foot and instantly regretted it. Not only did it send pain lancing up through her leg, but she figured that staggering about in sudden agony also diminished the imposing figure she had been trying to maintain.

Both fae-dragons reappeared, their laughter gone, expressions grim.

"There is no need for any of that shouting, nor your threats," Nevyk reprimanded. "You startled my young friend, and he came to fetch me. It appears we have made a foolish pact, but the laws of our court command that we uphold it. We will indeed take you to speak with Princess Jana. You may hang the lantern from that branch."

Placated, Echo hesitated. "I don't really want to lose my lantern."

"Will you accept a replacement?" Nevyk asked.

Thinking of the traces of iron in the lantern's frame, Echo shook her head.

Nevyk heaved an exasperated sigh. "Very well." A moment later, another lantern appeared, swinging from the branch he had indicated. The bit of blue flame melted away from the wick in Echo's lantern and drifted across to its new home. The fae-dragon glared at her. "Satisfied?"

"Yes."

"Good," Nevyk huffed. "Stand still."

Echo did as she was instructed. The dragons swooped around her in a dizzying pattern, their scales glinting in the light. She watched them until the pattern began to make her feel lightheaded, and then she squeezed her eyes tightly shut. For a moment, she experienced the sensation of falling, and when she opened her eyes again, the forest had disappeared. Now she stood in a small but comfortable room.

The walls were a polished, gnarled wood, and Echo realized that she must be inside the tree-tower. A small bed hung from the ceiling on the far side of the room, a filmy curtain of blue fabric draped on either side and tied with teal ribbons. To her left, a fireplace blazed merrily against the adjacent wall. Echo did not even try to figure out how that was possible without burning the tree down to the ground. Light streamed in through the window behind her. Echo glanced back and saw more gauzy blue curtains and a small, balconied veranda where a variety of beautiful potted flowers resided. To her right, in the center of the room, stood a table and two chairs, and against the back wall, next to the bed, a small vanity with a girl sitting before it, her head turned and a look of surprise on her face.

The girl was about Echo's age. Echo had always thought Mamai's hair was long, falling as it did to the small of her back, but this girl's hair pooled about the floor around her chair in a fiery waterfall. Echo guessed that when she stood, her hair probably still reached the floor. Large brown eyes identical to Mamai's stared out from a face so pale it seemed translucent. Dark circles hung beneath her eyes, and even in her surprise, she seemed weary to the point of exhaustion. Echo could not help but recognize the shape of Dadai's face in her features, and a pang rippled through her heart at the obvious resemblance. She wore a simple dress of shimmering blue with sleeves that ended above her elbows, though long points of fabric trailed down from her arms. White threads of fine embroidery adorned the bodice.

The orange dragon fluttered over to sit on the table next

to the girl. She stroked his back absently as she regarded her visitor.

"Who are you?" the girl asked.

"Princess Jana." Echo dropped her pack on the ground and gave a curtsy. She thought ruefully that it felt as though she had done nothing but curtsy since coming to Faerthain. She wished she was better at it. "My name is Echo."

Jana stared at her blankly.

"I…" Echo faltered, wishing Malilia were here with her. Surely the elf would have been able to help her explain. However, she had no choice but to stumble ahead. "I'm…" What could she say? To call herself the princess's sister might get her summarily expelled from the tower. But how could she explain quickly…? Something Malilia had told her sprang to mind and she spoke confidently, her mouth finding words she had heard her Mamai say to many patients over the years. "I understand that you are feeling poorly. I can help."

Jana brightened visibly. "Then you are most welcome here!" She nodded to Nevyk. "You are dismissed, milord."

Nevyk vanished without a ripple, leaving his counterpart still curled up on the vanity beneath Jana's hand. The princess smiled at Echo, her expression open and amicable. "My mother has sent so many to try to help, but none of them can tell me what is wrong. I still have hope, however," Jana said, her voice faint, though her eyes glowed with an intense faith Echo did not know how to respond to. "Please, sit. I will tell you my symptoms."

Echo obeyed, wondering how to get Drayeth to leave, too. "The dragon?" she asked. "Will he be staying?"

Jana tickled the little dragon under his chin. "Drayeth has

been my companion my whole life. His egg was a gift from one of my many goodmothers."

"Godmothers?" Echo asked, wondering that the fae would have such a custom.

A flicker of confusion crossed Jana's face. "No, good-mothers. And goodfathers. They are strong fae in my parents' court. Many of them brought pledge gifts to me when I was presented to the court as an infant. They are bound to protect me; some symbol of that duty is required. Drayeth hatched when I was a year old, and we have been the best of friends ever since."

"I see." Echo's mind raced over this new information. So, Drayeth was more than just a guardian appointed by the queen; perhaps he could be persuaded to help. His willing-ness to divulge the path to the Everflame glade suddenly made much more sense. "You were going to tell me about your symptoms."

Jana nodded, her expression grave. "I can't sleep. And everything I eat makes me feel nauseated. I feel..." She paused and placed a hand over her chest. "It is like there is a string tied around my ribs right here, and I can feel it pulling at me... like a longing for something."

"For what?" Echo asked.

"I do not know!" Jana's hands fell into her lap and she stared down at them. "My mother fears I am going insane; that is why she has locked me away up here. If the court thought my mind had grown unstable... it could cause a coup. I am the only heir to the throne."

"But aren't the fae immortal?" The question popped out before Echo could think better of it.

Jana's brow furrowed. "Umm... yes? What do you mean? You said that like you aren't one." She peered into Echo's eyes, then sat back, her delicate features puzzled. "A strong line of succession grants stability to the realm. Immortality has nothing to do with it."

"Of course." Echo waved a hand dismissively, hoping that it appeared to be a mere miscommunication. "Any other symptoms?"

Jana hesitated.

"Tell her," Drayeth urged.

Jana stared at him. "What? But... but you've always said I shouldn't tell anyone about them!"

"This one is different."

"How?"

"I'm not sure." Drayeth's wings flattened against his back. "But when I spoke with her before, she said something that made me trust her. I think you should, too. I don't think this one was sent by your mother. I think she might be safe."

"Tell me what?" Echo asked.

Jana picked up a glittering brooch off her table and began fidgeting with it. "I... I haven't told this to any of the others. But... I've been having this dream."

"Dreams?" Echo asked. "Are they part of the symptoms you've been having?"

"No... well... I don't know. It..." With precise care, Jana set the brooch back down. "Not dreams; that isn't precise. It's just one dream. I've been having it every night for as long as I can remember, possibly every night of my life. In it, I am very young, possibly an infant. I cannot speak in my dream, or move myself around. I have tried. I can usually manipulate my dreams, see them from different angles, change them... I can't do that in this one."

"What happens in the dream?" Echo asked.

"I am with my parents. They are holding me and talking

to me. My mother is singing, my father is laughing. I cannot understand their words, but I can feel their love. And there is this sound, a rhythmic, watery sound that fascinates and soothes me. When I wake"—tears glistened in Jana's eyes—"I can't even breathe! That is when that invisible cord pulls at me most insistently. It is like a longing, a yearning for something, but I do not know what I am longing for!"

Echo reached out and caught Jana's hands in her own. "I do," she whispered, suddenly finding a rush of words. "It is the sea you long for with such urgency. It is your heritage, and it calls you back to it. You must return to it or you will die. Please, you must come with me."

Jana stared at her with wide, frightened eyes and recoiled, tugging her hands violently from Echo's grasp. "The sea? What... no, that is impossible! I cannot leave here!" Her voice climbed to a shrill, panicked note. "I have to stay here, I have to get well again!"

"You will not get well if you stay here," Echo insisted.

Jana stood and whirled. With a few steps she had crossed the room and dived into her bed, the dark blue quilt pulled up over her head.

Echo rolled her eyes. This could not be happening. Surely there had been some mistake. This could not be the true daughter of her own, courageous parents. She followed the other girl and tugged the covers, but Jana fought her. However, the Summer Princess was in no condition to win at tug-of-war and after a bit of wrestling, Echo found herself staggering backwards across the room, the blanket bundled up in her arms.

"Jana!" she shouted, just barely stopping herself from stomping her foot again. "Listen to me! Your illness is treatable, but you have to listen!"

Jana sat up, her mussed hair flowing around her in waves and spreading out across the bed like a second blanket. She sniffled. "You can't treat me like this. I'm a princess! Drayeth, make her go away."

The little dragon fluttered near the bed, his head swinging this way and that, plainly torn.

Echo made an exasperated noise in her throat. She had imagined this going differently, and the ill temper of being famished, sleep-deprived, and in constant pain had certainly not been diminished by this reception. She lowered herself in a deeply exaggerated, mocking bow, holding the blanket out to one side like a cape.

"Forgive me, Your Highness. I'm only trying to save your life." Then, the sarcasm out of her system, Echo sighed and limped over to the bed, holding the blanket out as a peace offering.

Jana snatched the blanket and pulled it up around her chin, but she stayed upright, her eyes wary as Echo sat down on the edge of the bed with a grimace.

"I have a story to tell you," she began.

A FRIENDSHIP BEGINS

Though Echo stumbled through the unlikely tale, fumbling for words and telling some parts out of order and then having to correct herself and go back, Jana sat at perfect, silent attention. This unwavering regard might have inspired another storyteller, but it only served to further unnerve Echo. When the last, pathetically staggering word had limped out of her mouth, Echo stared at her hands, an uncomfortable and familiar heat rising in her ears. Now that she'd said it out loud, it sounded hollow and utterly unbelievable, even though she couldn't precisely remember a single word she had said. At no point had Jana given her any hint of whether she believed the story or of what she might be thinking. Echo fidgeted with a fold of her dress, waiting to hear the princess command Drayeth to throw her out again.

Instead, Jana leaned forward. "You are injured," she said. "Is that where the Winter King clawed you?"

Echo followed her gaze and realized that she was looking at the bandages on her back. Wordlessly, she nodded.

"Is he very terrible?" Jana asked.

Echo nodded, wrapping her arms around herself as she remembered his sharp claws and teeth.

Jana bit her lip. "You must love your parents very much, to do all this for them. You said you brought this... sealskin... with you? May I see it?"

Echo retrieved her pack and dug down to the bottom. She held up the tiny skin to the princess, who stared at it for a long, unblinking moment. Jana stretched her arm out, her hand hovering above the soft fur as if she might touch it, but then she shuddered and turned her head.

"Put it away."

Mystified, Echo obeyed.

Jana turned back to face her. "You must understand, the sea-fae are... they are not our enemies, exactly, but we are separate from them. Theirs is a court ungoverned by either the Summer or Winter regents, and as such, I have always been taught that they are dangerous and undisciplined. The... uncouth might say barbaric. To discover that I might be one of them"—her eyes flicked to Drayeth and back—"is difficult to accept."

"I understand more than you know," Echo said fervently. "Up until... two days ago? I've lost track of time here—I thought I was a normal human with normal human parents. I still don't even know what it means to be a wood-elf. I don't know how all of this is going to change your life. I don't even know how it's going to change mine. But I do know that if... if you don't get to the sea before the first day of summer, you will die."

Jana stared at the wall, her eyes unfocused. At length, she nodded. "I will come with you. But we must be careful. If my parents find out I have left the tower, they will be furious."

"They would stop you from being cured?"

"Not as such. But they would not believe your story." Jana turned to the fae-dragon. "Drayeth, can you get us out without Nevyk knowing we have gone?"

The flame-colored dragon bared his teeth. "Well... I'm not sure. But I can make it seem that you are still here in case he decides to come check on you. The illusion will hold unless he tries to touch it."

"How are we going to get out of here, then?" Echo asked, slumping wearily into a comfortable armchair and closing her eyes. She wished she could just take a short nap.

"We'll have to climb down," Jana said, a sudden gleam in her eye.

Echo appreciated this sudden display of gumption, but she did not think it the most practical solution. "I thought about trying to climb up earlier. There are vines growing around the tower, but they only reach about a third of the way up. There's nothing to hang onto; we'll fall to our deaths."

"We could cut my hair and twist it into a rope!" Jana declared. Echo opened her eyes to explain how ridiculous that sounded, just in time to see Jana snatch up a pair of sewing shears from a basket.

"Jana..."

But before she could get out another word, Jana had taken her hair in her hands and was chopping through her luxurious hair, letting it fall like a fiery waterfall in pools on the ground. Echo gaped in helpless amazement at the girl's impetuous gesture, as the shorn princess turned to smile at her.

"Oh... princess..." Echo breathed, then doubled over in a

fit of giggles. The sight of Jana's shortened hair sticking out from her head in a ragged line, mixed with her own exhaustion and fear, were too much for her to take.

"What's so funny?" Jana asked, her tone bewildered.

Echo laughed harder. When she finally managed to get her breath, she shook her head. "I was just going to ask, aren't there stairs somewhere?"

Two sets of eyes fixed unblinkingly upon her.

"Well? How did you get up here in the first place?" Echo asked.

"My parents brought me. Their power requires no stairs, and my illness necessitated a location I could not easily sleep-walk out of. Come on, help me gather this up and we'll braid it into a rope."

Echo looked at the mass of hair on the floor, then back up into Jana's earnest eyes. "Only if you let me trim your hair a bit more so it doesn't look so..." Echo circled a hand, searching for a word that would not offend and finding none.

Jana rose and went to her mirror, where her bewildered expression turned into one of amusement. "Ah," she began to giggle, "I see." She turned the shears over to Echo. "My lady."

Echo staggered to her feet and gave a wobbly curtsy as she accepted the shears. She set to work on Jana's hair, doing what she could to make it look a little more presentable.

Then they sat on the floor and began to gather up strands of the hair, braiding them together into a sturdy rope. As they braided, they talked. Or rather, Jana talked. Echo mostly listened, content to let Jana carry the conversation.

At last they had a sizable length of hair-rope, and together they lowered it over the balcony. To Echo's dismay, the braid only reached halfway down the tree, its end dangling far too high off the ground. It wouldn't even get them to the vines twining up the trunk.

"Perhaps there is a door," Echo muttered, "and stairs. Somewhere?"

"I've never seen one," Jana replied. "But I suppose it's possible."

Echo sighed. "You check the walls, especially behind the furniture. I'll take the floor."

"Check the walls? For what?" Jana stared at her.

"For a hidden door, of course," Echo barked, her patience running out. "There has to be one somewhere. There's always a hidden door."

Jana gave her a wide-eyed look of admiration. "Have you been in many situations like this?"

The question took her aback. "Er... no."

"But you've found a hidden door before?" Jana bounced on the bed a little, interest lighting her face and banishing a little of the pinched look of illness.

"Well... yes, actually," Echo said, thinking of how she had found the selkie skins in the first place. It had been mostly by accident, but Jana didn't need to know that. "Come on, help me."

They spent the next while scouring the room. Echo dug at every floorboard, but all of them were tightly fixed. Jana had no luck with the walls, either, though the search seemed to infuse a bit of vitality back into her. Echo sat on the floor and put her head in her hands, not wanting to admit defeat, but the truth could not be denied: they were trapped. After everything she had gone through, it was intolerable to be defeated by the lack of a staircase. Her thoughts returned to her first hour in Faerthain. The house Malilia had taken her to had been not unlike this one, a sort of dwelling carved into a trunk. But that one had stairs.

Wearily, Echo pushed herself up and went to look over the balcony once more, hoping to see something she had missed. But the tree still bore no steps, no ladder, no method of descent. The vines clinging to the tree gleamed verdant in the sunshine, tantalizingly close, and yet too far to reach. Echo eyed them. If only they were a little closer, if only... She closed her eyes and sighed, bowing her head to the railing.

A moment later, a startled yelp behind her made her jerk her head up to face Jana, who was gaping at her, or rather, past her.

"How are you doing that?" Jana exclaimed.

Echo frowned. "Doing what?"

Jana gestured, her hands waving in unintelligible circles. Echo turned around and reeled back, stumbling in her haste as a mass of ivy curled up over the balcony and began to spill onto the veranda.

"What? What...?" she spluttered.

"Make it stop!" Jana shouted, as the vines continued to creep toward them.

"What do you mean, 'make it stop'?" Echo yelled back. "I'm not doing this!"

"Of course you are!"

"No, I'm not!"

"If it's not you, then who? Make it stop!" Jana commanded.

Echo stared at the oncoming growth, backing away from the overhang. She had just been wishing they were more accessible, but could this really be her own doing? The ivy already wound halfway across the floor and it was stretching ever higher. If this didn't stop soon they would be closed into the room and—eventually—crushed. Echo held up her hands.

"Stop!" she shouted in the most imperious tone she could muster.

The growth continued, tendrils crawling toward her.

"Stop!" Her voice sounded less commanding and more panicked this time.

Still no change.

"Please stop?" she begged.

Jana screamed. Echo dashed over to the bed and retrieved her pack, then grabbed the princess by the arm, pulling her toward the rapidly clogging doorway.

"Come on!" she shouted. "We have to climb down!"

"But, but—!" Jana protested, tugging her arm away from Echo's grasp. "But I can't!"

"Look, I don't have time to argue with you. Drayeth and I will help you climb down, but we have to go now or we'll be trapped."

"I... I..."

"A moment ago you wanted to make a rope out of your own hair to climb down," Echo reminded her, indicating the braid still hanging from the railing. "This will be easier than that, I promise!"

Jana took a deep breath and seemed to find a spark of courage, for she nodded and allowed herself to be led across the room. They picked their way over the thick tendrils that were now beginning to curl their way around the furniture. The doorway was filled with leaves, and ivy spiraled around the doorframe, hanging down like a curtain. Echo pushed her way through, trying not to harm the vines. If they had come to life of their own accord, she did not wish to anger them by cutting her way out.

She had begun to swing her leg over the now-buried railing when Jana let out a cry and stumbled. Looking over her shoulder, Echo could see that the princess was stuck back in the doorway. Gritting her teeth, she pulled out her knife and brandished it like a sword as she scrambled over the writhing carpet and sliced into the vines restraining Jana.

"Hurry, hurry!" she urged Echo, whimpering as she pulled at her captured foot.

"I'm trying!" Echo snapped, utterly exasperated and starting to wonder if she'd come all this way just to be defeated by a bunch of magical plants.

At last, though, she was through and Jana's foot came free.

"Over the railing! Quick!" Echo directed.

Bundling up her skirts, Jana threw her leg over the railing and clung to one of the thicker vines, her face white with terror. Echo followed after her, shinnying down with ease. However, when she looked up, she saw Jana still stationary, Drayeth fluttering about her head in distress. With a sigh, Echo hauled herself back up until she rested just below the other girl.

"Jana? I'm right here, Jana," she called, trying to emulate a soothing cadence she'd heard her father use when she was younger. "You can do this. I'm right here, and Drayeth is right here, and together we are not going to let you fall. Right, Drayeth?"

The little dragon made a nervous sound of affirmation.

"Good." She pulled the sturdy braid of hair over and

pressed it into Jana's hands. "You need to wrap your hands around the rope and reach your left foot down about six inches. There's a loop of vines there you can rest in. Can you do that, Jana?"

"I... I think so." Jana's voice was shaky. Slowly, she unhooked her toes and stretched down until she felt the loop Echo had described.

"Good job, Jana!" Echo praised. "Now, this will be harder: you need to rest your weight on that foot, and use our rope to lower yourself down so we can do it again. You can do it; I'm still right here."

Jana made a frightened sound, but a moment later Echo could see her moving. They continued their descent in this fashion, Echo maintaining a steady stream of calm, encouraging words mingled with precise instruction. Thankfully, the vines were so thick and plentiful that the descent was otherwise straightforward, and at long last they alighted on the blessedly stationary ground. Jana stepped away and tilted her head back, staring up at the tree they had just climbed down, her face even whiter than before.

"I... I..." She shook her head then turned to Echo. "Thank you. I could not have done that without you." She sank to the ground as though she had expended all her energy in the climb.

"Ah, well. My... uh, well, Dadai... he talked like that to me once." Echo's feet hurt so she sat down next to Jana. The bandages had gotten pushed askew in the climb and a few of the cuts had reopened and were seeping blood. She worked to adjust the position of the cloths. "I had climbed a tree and when I realized how high I'd gotten I was too scared to come down."

Jana looked like she wanted to respond to that, but didn't

know how. After an uncomfortable pause, she said, "Well... I have never been forced to brave such perils. Is everyone in the mortal realm accustomed to such treacherous circumstances?"

Echo blinked. "You mean climbing out of towers about to be overrun by plants that appear to have come to life on their own and are intent on crushing you? Er... no. That's more fae-realm stuff, if you ask me."

Jana waved a hand. "I only meant the climbing part. You appear to be proficient in such skills; I have a difficult time imagining you being afraid of heights now."

Echo yawned. How long had it been since she last slept? "No. I mean, well, I have gotten a lot more experience since then. Climbing trees is something a lot of children do. And Dadai has let me climb about in the rigging of various ships when they're in port and not being loaded. Usually while wearing a harness, though, and not even the mainmast is that high, but height isn't really the problem."

"I see." Jana nodded seriously, as though she really did see. Impetuously, she embraced Echo, then stepped back, her face alight with a mischievous grin. "I've always wanted a sister," she declared. "I'm glad I got one like you."

Echo smiled uncomfortably at her and pretended to survey the surrounding forest. Though she had thought of Jana as sister since the moment she had heard about her, and even called her that to others, hearing the princess say it suddenly left a bitter taste in her mouth. "Anyway, now that we're out of the tower, any chance you know where we can find a door to the mortal realm?"

Jana adopted a serious expression. "I know the locations of all portals within my domain."

"Great. Where's the closest one?"

Jana pointed into the wood. "The Celshike circle stones are the closest gate, but…"

Echo nodded. "Perfect. Let's go." With some effort, she rose, slowly striding in the direction Jana had pointed.

"But…" Jana followed her, trotting and stumbling a bit in her attempts to keep up.

Echo didn't wait. She was tired, and she was fed up with the alien, unpredictable world of fae. At the moment, she did not care that Faerthain held her actual heritage, nor did she harbor any curiosity to explore it further. All she knew was that she had experienced more than enough danger and excitement over the past two days—or however long it had been—to last her a lifetime. She wanted to go home, sleep in her own bed, do her chores, and eat her mother's cooking. If the past few days had taught her anything, it was that she much preferred going on adventures when they were contained within the pages of a book.

After only a few minutes' walk, she spotted a ring of massive pillars, inscribed with runes she could not read. The weathered gray stones stood a dozen strong, sentinels with ancient trees growing between them and twining branches overhead. Across the Celshike circle, Echo glimpsed a small opening in the farthest pillar, like a doorway. She beckoned impatiently to Jana, who had fallen behind and was doubled over, breathing hard.

Echo had endured so much, but finally, finally, she was going home. Jana might not be everything she'd expected, but her parents would be overjoyed to have their daughter back, and who could say? Perhaps they could even grow to become friends. For all her quaking, Jana had come along gamely with barely a protest; maybe once she had her strength back she'd be rather a lot of fun.

Echo pointed. "Is that the door?"

"Yes," Jana panted. "But... I need to..."

"Then what are we waiting for?" Echo seized the other girl's wrist and plunged through the opening, dragging the princess along behind her.

21

THE WINTER REALM

The first thought Echo could muster was that it was cold. But "cold" lacked a crucial intensity. No, this was not merely cold. The wintry wind raked at every bit of exposed skin with needle-sharp teeth. She blinked rapidly, certain that the small amount of liquid in her eyes would freeze if exposed to the air for too long. The cuts on her feet throbbed with an icy ache that sliced all the way to her bones; she looked down to see that she stood ankle-deep in snow. They were standing amidst a ring of stones similar to the Faerthain circle, but the markings were different, and the landscape was utterly barren of trees. Flakes of snow drifted around them, stirred up by the breeze that swept across the tundra.

"This... this can't be right. It's almost summer in the mortal realm; we can't have been gone this long!" Echo swung around, her eyes sweeping across the rolling hills blanketed in snow. Jana shuddered violently, her wrist still clutched in Echo's hand. Her presence calmed the surging panic; if Jana was still alive, then there was still time until the summer solstice. They were merely in the wrong location. But... where was that?

Jana's teeth chattered. "I t-tried to t-tell you," she said, tugging her wrist from Echo's grip and rubbing her arms. "Y-you have to align the door before you go through. The C-Celshike d-door opens to multiple realms." She glanced over her shoulder. "Wait! Where's Drayeth?"

Echo scanned the area, but saw no sign of the little orange dragon. "Maybe he didn't come through with us?"

"He never leaves my side; something must have happened to him! We have to look for him!" The hysteria in Jana's voice escalated with every word.

"Don't worry, we'll find him. He was right behind us; maybe he went to do some scouting." Echo tried to calm the princess. "Do you have any idea where we are?" Echo asked, trying to distract her.

Jana stamped her feet and Echo noticed that she, also, was barefoot. "M-my guess would be Vetirheim, the Winter Realm."

"Your guess would be accurate, little ones." A tall, lithe figure stepped out from behind a stone. He was pale, with raven-black hair and icy blue eyes and looked only a little older than herself. But what caught Echo's attention most were the sleek, black-feathered wings jutting from his back.

Jana huddled closer to Echo with a slight whimper. "A rifinn," she whispered. Echo had no idea what that meant, but she had no time to ask questions.

"Forgive us, we meant no trespass," Echo said, trying to keep her voice from trembling, either from fear or cold. "I did not realize the door was not aligned properly."

The man smiled and waved a hand. "All is forgiven."

More figures stepped out from behind the stones, and

with each new arrival Echo's heart sped up, pounding a frantic rhythm meant for flight. Run! But her feet were rooted in place as the figures emerged—a lion with ebony fur and giant wings sprouting from between its shoulder blades; a short creature that looked halfway between a man and a mole with a squat, oval face and a mouth full of tiny, sharp teeth; an enormous black wolf; and a girl about her own size but with pure white hair and sharply pointed ears. It was the man with the wings, however, who made her quake with fear. The others did not possess the same intimidating presence nor exude that casual confidence that surrounded him like a cloak.

"Our thanks," Echo said, trying not to stare at the creatures surrounding them. "Then we'll just be going."

"Oh." The man's features drooped in a sympathetic expression of regret, though his icy eyes retained a cocksure amusement. "I am afraid that simply isn't possible. You see, the Celshike circle does not open from this side. It is the unfortunate side effect of having a gate powerful enough to take you anywhere."

Echo glanced at Jana. "Is that true?" she whispered.

Jana gave a tight nod.

The man rubbed his finger just beneath his ear, adopting a thoughtful mien. "You do not appear dressed for our realm. Please, allow us to extend you our hospitality. Perhaps we can help you find a door that will take you to the place you wished to go."

Echo frowned. "I know nothing of you or your companions, not even what you are. How do I know you do not intend us harm?"

He spread his arms, and his wings extended slightly behind him. "We are the keepers of the Celshike gate. So long as you mean our realm no harm, we mean you none. Please, accept our most gracious offer before you both freeze to death where you stand. Vetirheim is no place to go wandering about barefoot."

"The fae cannot lie," Jana whispered. "But they can speak in riddles, and they can omit the truth."

"If we don't reach the mortal realm by the summer solstice, my companion will die," Echo said. She heard Jana's sharp intake of breath and hoped she would keep quiet. It was a calculated risk, telling them this, but one she felt might be necessary, in case they considered lifetime imprisonment to fall under the category of "no harm."

His eyes narrowed. "Is that so? Well, that shouldn't be a problem."

Echo did not like the sound of that. Did he mean that they could get to a gate in time, or that he simply didn't care and therefore it wasn't a problem for him if Jana died? Her teeth were beginning to chatter from the cold. "C-can you take us to a gate that will send us to the mortal realm? That's where we meant to go."

"Perhaps," the young man mused.

"We will only come with you if you give me your name," Echo announced, remembering what Malilia had implied about the fae and their names.

This seemed to both startle and amuse him, for his stony expression wavered momentarily and his lips twitched. He regarded her for a long, silent moment, then gave a shallow bow. "My name is Eirloch, and as your friend has correctly surmised, I am a rifinn. I am at your service, my lady. But come, we must get you both out of this snow before the frost damages your feet beyond repair."

Echo glanced inquisitively at Jana, who gave a helpless

little shrug. Eirloch turned, and they had little choice but to follow. Outside the Celshike stones, the drifts grew deeper and every step felt like it might be her last. Echo kept glancing at Jana, impressed by her stoic endurance. Other than the shivers that wracked her body, the Summer Princess gave no outward indication that she even felt the snow. Determined to match her fortitude, Echo bit back her own shivers. The cold was better than the obsidian shards, but not by much.

The walk was blessedly short. They crested a hill just outside the circle, and a large cottage rose up to greet them, its many windows lit by the pleasant amber glow of a hearth. Eirloch opened the door and led them into a spacious foyer. Warmth wrapped Echo in a fond embrace as the white-haired girl shut the door behind them.

"Maeva, we're home! We've brought visitors!" Eirloch called.

A woman emerged from a side room. A quick glance confirmed that she was another rifinn, though her hair was silver and wound into a tight bun. Her wings were covered in soft, silvery feathers. She eyed Echo and Jana, her gray eyes suspicious.

"Where did you find them? They do not look to be of Vetirheim."

"They are not; they came through the Celshike door. Apparently they ended up here by accident."

Maeva turned sharply. "Eirloch! Your job is to guard the gate, not to bring home strays. How do you expect to ever advance in rank if you neglect your duties? These trespassers should be taken to His Majesty."

"Look at them. They will not survive the trip dressed as they are."

"They should have thought of that before they entered our realm."

"Mother," Eirloch began, then stopped with a sigh. "You are right. But I already promised that no harm would come to them."

"You what?" the older woman hissed.

"I can take them to the king, but I can't trudge them through the snow without shoes on. I gave my name."

Maeva spun on her heel and disappeared.

Eirloch grimaced. "I knew she wouldn't be happy about this." He glared at Echo. "I don't know why I didn't just take you to the Winter King immediately. I didn't need your permission."

Echo had been thinking along the same lines, but she gave him the most innocent smile she could. "Something smells wonderful," was all she said.

The rifinn sighed. He made a dismissive gesture and his companions departed, disappearing down a corridor to their left. Then he beckoned to the two girls.

"Come along, you might as well have some warm stew while I try to figure out what to do with you."

Maeva stood in the room they entered, angrily pounding a lump of dough with her fists. She looked up when they entered, and Echo thought she saw her expression suddenly shift from fury to cunning. Echo accepted a bowl of stew from Eirloch, but kept one eye on Maeva. Would the stew bind her to these fae if she ate it? These were Winter Court fae, and it might not be as safe for her. A glance at Jana confirmed this worry; the princess held the warm bowl between her hands but made no effort to pick up the spoon.

"Eirloch," Maeva said, her voice turning grumpy again, "if

they're not interested in food, then get them out of my kitchen."

"Why don't you put them in the guest room?" Eirloch suggested.

A dull warning sounded in Echo's mind, but exhaustion hung from her eyelids like the weights Dadai sewed into his nets. Her mind spun and the world blurred. How long since she had last slept? Right now, the thing she wanted most was a warm, soft bed, though she would have just as gladly taken a cold, hard floor. She just wanted to be left alone for a few hours to sleep. So when Eirloch offered to show them to a place where they could stay for the night, she did not argue.

He led them upstairs to a spacious room with several simple pallets of animal skins. Warmth radiated from the hearth in which a merry fire already danced. A tiny window opposite the door looked out over the white landscape, though Echo noticed that it had no mechanism whereby it could be opened. A large chest of drawers stood next to the door, looking lonely without any other furniture around it. The woodpile took up a large portion of one wall.

"Should you need anything during the night, just call out to me or Maeva," Eirloch said. "I hope you rest well here."

The two girls entered the room and Eirloch pulled the door closed behind him as he left.

"I don't like this," Jana whispered.

"Neither do I. But I don't know how to get us out of this."

Jana's face grew pale. "We are in Vetirheim," she whispered. "I shouldn't be here at all."

Echo's back twinged at the memory of the tiger's claws. "It's a good thing you don't exactly look like royalty," Echo whispered back, indicating Jana's scraggly locks. "But at least we have a safe place to sleep for now. You should lie down and try to get some rest." In truth, the princess looked as though she might collapse at any moment and Echo worried for every minute that brought them closer to summer.

Jana nodded and obediently curled up on one of the pallets. Echo draped a fur over her, helping the princess pull it up to her chin. Jana closed her eyes and a moment later, her breathing grew deep and even. Wearily, Echo went to the door and tried the latch, something she had not wanted to do while Jana was still awake. As she had expected, she found it locked, but she was too tired to feel any fear. There would be time enough for that tomorrow. At least Jana would not be able to sleepwalk out of the room and into the snow. Wearily, she sank into her own pile of furs. A wellspring of homesickness coursed through her body as she lay there, relaxing into the softness of the bed.

"Creator," she whispered into the quiet of the room, "please be with Mamai and Dadai. Prevent them from worrying too much. And give me strength and the courage I need to finish this quest and bring my sister home to them. I cannot do it on my own."

With this prayer still fresh on her lips, Echo sank into the peaceful oblivion of sleep.

22

AN IMPOSSIBLE TASK

*E*cho's nose was cold. She wrinkled it slightly as she blinked her eyes open. An early gray light lit the small window. The fire had died down in the hearth, and though the furs kept the rest of her warm, she could see her breath steaming in the air. She cast a worried look over at the lump that was Jana snuggled down on the other pallet. She could see the furs rising and falling with each breath Jana took, and Echo blew out a quiet sigh of relief. However, she did not think this cold would improve Jana's condition, so she got up, wrapping a long fur blanket around herself like a cloak. The floorboards were like ice beneath her bare feet, but she gritted her teeth and padded over to the hearth where a few embers still glowed feebly.

She stirred up the coals and began feeding it kindling. The flames reacted sluggishly, as though they had no wish to rise early, but eventually she got them to flare sufficiently that when she added a few logs the fire lapped at them hungrily. Warmth began to permeate the room, but Jana continued to sleep.

A flutter of fear coursed through Echo's veins. How much time did she have left? She tried to assemble a timeline of events, but she had spent so much of her time traveling between realms that she wasn't sure if she really had the four days she calculated. She wished her parents were here, or even Malilia. She tried to wake Jana, and the princess stirred and sat up, her eyes glassy with sleep. Echo put a hand to the princess's forehead and frowned.

"You feel a bit feverish."

The princess stared at her, a confused look in her eyes. "Where are we?"

"In Vetirheim, remember?"

"Vetir... oh, right. I hoped perhaps all that had been a dream. Are we prisoners?"

"I'm not sure," Echo said. "The door is locked."

"Try knocking on it," Jana suggested. "If nothing else, it might remind them to feed us."

Echo's stomach rumbled, and since she had no better ideas, she went to the door and rapped on it as loudly as she could. The soft thudding sound did not seem to go far; the door was thick and solid and she had no idea of whether or not anyone might have been close enough to hear her, but it felt good to have done something.

She sat down on Jana's pallet and opened her pack. Little food remained within: a meat pie, a few muffins, and three apples. They split the meat pie, polishing it off with haste born of hunger. Echo was just debating on whether they should more carefully ration the rest of her supplies when the door swung open. Eirloch appeared with a tray of food, which he set on the floor. Then he seated himself next to it, beckoning for them to join him. Echo grabbed a couple of furs from their beds and set them on the ground, not wishing for Jana to get chilled on the cold floor.

There were bowls of muesli topped with dried berries, a pitcher of cream, slices of smoked fish, cubes of cheese, and rye bread with an assortment of jams. Good fare, and with a delicious aroma, but it was so different from Mamai's breakfasts. A great pang of homesickness struck Echo deep inside, and she felt as though she were a harp whose string has just been plucked and found to be sadly out of tune. She lowered her eyes and breathed a silent plea for help getting home.

"You may eat without fear," Eirloch said with a grin. "I noticed you both left your stew untouched last night. On my name, I swear that this food has no binding upon it. Besides, it is clear that both of you are Summer Fae. Our courts are not so different that this would affect you the same as it would a mortal." As if to demonstrate his integrity, he lifted a slice of bread and began coating it with a thick helping of blackberry preserves.

Jana chose an assortment of bread and cheese and began to nibble daintily. Echo hesitated, but Malilia had indicated that her fae heritage should protect her. Her stomach growled, deciding for her, and she reached for the food.

"I have thought of a way that you can show us your thanks," Eirloch announced as they ate.

"What?" Echo nearly dropped her spoonful of muesli; the oats were too finely chopped for her taste, but the dried fruit helped with the texture. "Excuse me?"

Eirloch raised his eyebrows. "My friends and I did save you from freezing to death when you came through the Celshike gate. If we hadn't brought you home with us..."

"Kidnapped us, you mean," Echo grumbled.

Eirloch continued as if he hadn't heard her, "You'd be

Summer Court ice statues by now. We only ask that you complete one simple task for us in payment."

"You avowed that no harm would come to us," Jana reminded him, her tone imperious.

"And none shall," Eirloch assured her. "The task we have in mind poses no danger to either of you."

"My friend has to return to the mortal realm before the summer solstice or she will die. That would be harmful," Echo argued.

"You have four days until then," Eirloch said with a wide grin. "Plenty of time."

Echo narrowed her eyes at him. Internally, she was glad that her calculations had been correct, but she did not wish to let him see her relief. "If we do this task, will you take us to the nearest gate to the mortal realm?"

Eirloch chuckled. "That depends on how well you solve our problem."

"Your problem?" Jana asked.

The young rifinn sighed dramatically. "My companions and I are young, and as such, we are currently the lowest ranking members of His Majesty's guard. That is why we have been assigned to keep watch over a gate that sees little use."

"That must be difficult," Jana replied diplomatically.

Echo could not prevent herself from rolling her eyes, but Eirloch did not seem to notice.

"It is," he replied. "While we are well-equipped for the cold, our shifts of standing in the snow are tiresome."

"Just tell us what you want," Echo burst out.

Eirloch's lips twitched at her impatience. "It is simple, really."

"So you've said." Echo crossed her arms and frowned at him. "And yet you won't just come out and say it."

"You're a perceptive one. Very well, I shall stop circling the snowbank, as we say." He rose and opened the door and his four companions entered the room. He gestured to them collectively. "We need a chair."

Echo lowered her eyebrows in a puzzled frown.

"We keep our post alone," Eirloch continued. "And we don't want to have to haul chairs back and forth. So what we want is simple: a single chair that is comfortable for all of us."

There it was. Echo's spirits plummeted as she surveyed the five fae. They were each so vastly different in size and shape; what kind of chair could possibly accommodate them all?

"What you ask is impossible," she whispered, her voice stolen along with her hope.

"You may use the logs, or anything else you can find in this room," Eirloch continued, ignoring her dismay. "If you need tools or anything else to help you construct the chair, you may ask for it. If it is within our power, we will grant it. There should be some whittling tools in the dresser."

With that, he and the other creatures left the room. Echo heard the bolt slide into place, locking them in.

A scream of rage and frustration bubbled up out of her throat and exploded into the empty room, sounding loud and hollow as it bounced off the bare walls. She flew at the door and beat it with her fists, shouting wordlessly after them, driving all her fury into her cries. Every hurt she had endured, every moment of weariness, every fear she had faced brimmed up and flowed out of her mouth. Her hands bruised and her throat grew raw. When she had exhausted herself she slid down to her knees, her head bowed against the door.

"Perhaps we can do it."

The quiet voice behind her made Echo raise her head and glance dully at her companion. "What?"

"Perhaps we can do it," Jana repeated. "Make them the chair they want."

"Did you see them?" Echo demanded hoarsely. "One of them is a lion, with wings. Why he even wants a chair, I have no idea. Then there's three different sized people, and a wolf. How are we supposed to design a chair for any of them, let alone all of them?"

Jana looked down at her hands. "I'm sorry," she said, her voice soft. "I just... I don't think they'll let us out of here until we at least try."

Echo's fury faded into guilt. "You're right. We should"— she gestured at the pile of logs—"do something with that."

She rose and rummaged through the dresser drawers while Jana ate a little more. The search was less than satisfying, but did reveal a knife, two hatchets, an old saw with bent and broken teeth that would be worse than useless, a mallet, a tangle of string, and various other bits and pieces of things like broken pottery, feathers, and dead leaves. Bringing one of the hatchets to Jana, Echo chose a log at random and began hacking at it with the other small axe to remove the bark.

"Do you have any experience making furniture?" she asked the princess hopefully.

Jana shook her head, peering perplexedly at her chosen piece.

"Didn't think so," Echo muttered. "Well, neither do I. Though I've watched Dadai build a few smaller things. He usually starts with boards, though, not logs. I guess our first job should be to whittle these into boards? This... this is going to take forever."

Jana nodded quietly, chipping away at her log, and Echo resisted the urge to melt into a puddle of despair.

"How are you feeling?" she asked instead.

Jana coughed a little. "Tired," she admitted. "And cold."

"It's warmer by the fire," Echo suggested. "And you should wrap one of those furs around you while you work."

Jana did not argue as Echo urged her closer to the hearth and brought the log over for her. The two girls settled in by the fireplace, working in silence. The log Echo had chosen rested beneath her outstretched palm, stabilizing it against the floor the way she had seen her father do.

"Would you..." Jana trailed off, hesitant.

Echo looked up. "Yes?"

Jana looked down at her hands, fiddling with the haft of her hand axe. "I was just wondering... can you tell me about... your... parents?"

Echo faltered on her swing, glancing off the wood. For a moment she stared at the divot she'd created, then raised the hatchet again. It was only natural for Jana to want to know about them, but Echo's throat seemed to close over the words, as if speaking about her parents might somehow give a piece of them to Jana, and suddenly she found that she was loath to share them.

The bark chipped off in tiny, ragged flakes, and her blade caught on the corners, leaving a jagged, rough mark across the grain. She gritted her teeth. She had not expected the chore to be so difficult on her own. The few times she had begged to help, Dadai's hands had always been there, guiding hers.

How could she put her parents into words? How could she capture Dadai's gentle strength, or Mamai's warmth? How could she express their love?

A poisonous selfishness rose up within her, planted by Ritioghra's words: what if her return to her rightful place leaves you without one?

Angrily, she swung again, casting all her frustration and fear down with the shining blade in an attempt to dislodge the Winter King's venom, but this attempt went no more smoothly than the first. A depth of understanding emerged in her heart as she realized just how patient her father had always been in allowing her to "help." His teaching had always been so tender and kind, his encouragement sincere, but she now wondered how much more quickly he could have accomplished things had she been content to merely watch. And yet, he never seemed to begrudge the extra time or the teaching; in fact, he always seemed to enjoy it. Maybe that was something she could say, but... it wasn't enough. It wasn't the real full, truth of who he was.

She risked a quick glance at the princess, whose brow was furrowed in concentration. Words couldn't hope to suffice. And yet, she knew she had to try to answer, no matter how fumbling and insufficient her attempts might be. Jana deserved that much.

"Mamai is like the sun," Echo began, her hands moving as she talked. The thin shavings of wood were coming off in longer and longer strips as she found the rhythm of the work. "She is warm and kind to everyone. The villagers often ask for her when someone is sick or melancholy. She is always ready to help whoever she can, and she usually brings them a basket of scones while she's at it."

"She bakes?" Jana asked, still struggling with her own

blade. Her face was red, and she frowned as she studied Echo's motions.

"The most wonderful treats." Echo smiled. "Scones and biscuits and honey cakes and more. And they always taste amazing, and they look pretty, too. But it's more than that... she's cheerful to be around. There's a... a playfulness about her. When I was little, she would always make up games to play, things that made chores and rainy days more fun. She's not very tidy, though. She often forgets to make her bed." Echo grinned a little. "But sometimes she gets so sad." Echo's fingers stilled on the branch she held, a flutter of sorrow and fear gripping her stomach. Ritioghra's words rang again in her mind, taunting her trust in her parents, questioning her place in their home once Jana was restored to their arms. She scowled and began working furiously on the branch once more, shoving his words away. "And Dadai," she continued through gritted teeth, "he is like the moon. Strong and gentle and constant. Even when you can't see him, he's always there, watching out for us, working hard so that Mamai and I can have a home and good food and clothes. He works so hard, but he also knows how to play. He tells the best stories..." Echo trailed off, remembering the last story her father had told her, the night she had left him behind to enter Faerthain. Would he forgive her for entering the fae-realm alone?

"They sound lovely," Jana murmured.

"I can't do them justice. I can't wait for you to meet them. They've missed you so much."

Jana leaned over her hatchet, her auburn hair falling forward and hiding her face. "How could they miss me? They don't know me."

"They never stopped loving you," Echo said. "I didn't

notice it for many years. I was... young... too young to understand. But there's always been... a sorrow to them, even in their laughter, a hole nothing could fill. The place you were supposed to be."

"And yet... they raised you and loved you? Even though they knew you weren't their own?" Jana's voice held a touch of disbelief.

Echo looked down at the floor. "Yes." A rising tide of fierce love welled within her, dispelling the Winter King's poisonous words and quenching her own insecurities. "They chose to love me."

"Echo..." Jana glanced up from her work, her hands falling still. "When we get back... what am I supposed to do? I can't just stop being the Summer Princess. I mean... I don't think I can."

"I don't know. I just know that you need to get to the sea, or you won't just stop being the Summer Princess... you'll stop... being."

Jana nodded, biting her upper lip. She pulled the hatchet across the wood and a long, delicate shaving of wood curled off and drifted to the floor. She glanced up, and the two girls shared an accomplished grin. They worked in silence for a while before Jana spoke again.

"Echo?"

"Hm?"

Her voice dropped to a whisper. "I hope they like me."

23

JANA'S IDEA

*T*rying to plane logs into boards by hand was tedious, frustrating work. Then the branch she was working on snapped, and with it, Echo's patience. She cast the hatchet to the floor and rose, pacing the room and rubbing her sore hands. At the rate they were going, the chair might be finished by the middle of next year, and she still hadn't figured out how to design it so that all five of the young guardians would find it comfortable.

"We've been at this for hours and all we have to show for our work is a pile of shavings and sawdust!" Echo grimaced at Jana. "You've spent your entire life in Faerthain; do you have any ideas for this thing?"

Jana slumped against the fireplace with a shiver, pulling the fur tightly around her shoulders. "I thought you had a plan. I've just been following your lead."

An angry retort sprang to Echo's lips, but a look at Jana's white face killed it before she could utter the words. She hadn't exactly been transparent when they began this work; she supposed that she must have looked like she had a design in mind. With a sigh, she sank down onto the pile of furs that served as her bed.

"It's too bad we can't just pile up a bunch of furs," Jana said, giving a little laugh that sounded alarmingly like a cough. "That would be pretty comfortable for all of them."

"That's true, but they said they wanted a chair," Echo said, running her fingers glumly through the fibers of the soft fur beneath her. She shot upright. "Jana, you're a genius!" she exclaimed. "That's exactly what we'll do!"

"What?" Jana asked.

"You were right! We can make them a chair. It might not look like a chair, but a chair it shall be. We're going to need some help, though. And it's been a while since they fed us." Echo hopped up and strode to the door. She banged on it until it swung open to reveal Eirloch's smiling face.

"Yes? Can we get you anything?" he asked.

"I'm going to need some leather cords," Echo began, "long ones. And an awl. And I need you and your friends to come in here and help chop up all of this wood into the finest shavings you can."

Eirloch reared back slightly, startled at the force of her demands. "I can get you the leather and the awl. How long do you need the cords to be?"

"As long as you have," Echo said.

"But as for our help... the deal was that you would make the chair."

"You said that if I needed anything within your power to grant, I could ask for it and you'd give it to me."

Eirloch glanced sideways at Jana.

The princess nodded firmly. "You did say that. Unless your duties prevent you from assisting us—and you have already informed us that they do not, since you take turns guarding the gate—you are bound to give her what she asks."

"Spoken like the fae," Eirloch grumbled. "Very well. But, if I may ask, why should we destroy the very materials we have provided for the chair? Won't that make your task more difficult?"

Echo gave an airy shrug. "You'll just have to wait and see. Oh, and my friend needs some warm soup and more blankets."

Eirloch gave her a wry grin. "As you wish, my lady."

He closed the door behind him, and Echo crossed her arms, satisfaction making her want to jump and shout. For the first time all day, she felt like they might make it out of this cottage, and if they could make it through this trial, perhaps there was hope of getting home and saving Jana after all.

Eirloch returned bearing a bowl full of something thick and steaming, three of his friends trailing after him. Echo immediately took charge, instructing the young fae guardians to chop and plane the wood into sawdust. While they were doing that, she busied herself with the leather cords and the awl, working holes into the edges of the first fur on her pallet and stringing the cord through it. Jana sipped weakly at her soup and Echo kept a close eye on her.

They all worked late into the night until exhaustion overtook them and Echo finally called a halt.

"We all need rest," she announced. "But we start again with the dawn. We will need more logs, too. A lot more."

The wolf bared his teeth but nobody complained out loud as they retired to their own rooms. Jana had already fallen asleep, and Echo tucked her fur up around her chin, surveying their progress beneath heavy eyelids. They had accumulated a fairly sizable pile of sawdust and shavings, and she had already laced several furs together. She climbed onto her slightly diminished pallet and closed her eyes.

The sun peeked through her window all too soon and Echo dragged herself out of bed. Her arms and back were sore, her fingers red and swollen from the awl. And though her wounds had already begun to heal, the gashes in her feet and the claw marks from Ritioghra still ached when she moved or stepped wrong. Her stomach growled, reminding her that she had neglected to eat any supper the evening before. When Eirloch arrived with breakfast, it was all Echo could do to keep from diving at it like a bird of prey.

The day progressed much as the one before had. The pile of sawdust continued to grow and Echo darned more furs together. Jana had developed a slight fever in the night and Echo refused to let her get up and help, insisting that she stay in bed and drink plenty of warm tea.

The fae grinned cunningly as they destroyed the logs with knives and claws. Echo knew that they believed her foolish, for she had not explained her plan. To them, it appeared that she was wasting good material, but since her failure only meant that they would not have to uphold their end of the bargain, none of them complained. Only the white-haired girl gave any indication of concern for either of them, but she only expressed it by bringing a cool cloth for Jana's forehead and giving Echo sad, puzzled glances. Echo wished she could thank the girl for her ministrations, but since none of Eirloch's companions had offered a name, she felt awkward speaking to them.

The sun set and Eirloch and his companions retired once more. At the door, the rifinn paused.

"The gate to the mortal realm is a good day's journey

from here. I thought you should know. If you wish to reach the sea by the first day of summer, the chair needs to be finished by tomorrow."

Echo considered him for a long moment. "Why are you telling me this?"

"It seemed only fair," the young rifinn replied.

"I see. Thank you."

Eirloch bowed his head, his wings flaring slightly, and then he swept out, shutting the door softly behind him. Echo checked on Jana, but the princess was already asleep. The skin on her forehead felt hot to the touch, but Echo suppressed her worry. All she could do was focus on the task before her.

On her pallet, Jana mumbled and cried out in her sleep, tossing fitfully. Her covers slid down, and Echo hurried to replace them, lingering a precious moment over her sister's restless form.

"We're going home," she promised in a whisper. "I'm going to get you home."

All that night she worked, stopping only to stoke the fire and relieve the stiffness that set in after hours upon the floor. Her eyes ached, straining in the dim light, and her fingers grew raw and blistered against the stiff hides and the wooden handle of the awl. As the air grew colder, she was forced to pause more often to warm her cramping hands over the hearth, and all the while, she worried it would not be enough, that she would not be finished in time.

Would dawn never come? And yet, Echo had no wish to hasten the time as it passed. She needed every minute she had to complete the task before her.

Eventually, just as the light began to break across the horizon, Echo finished tying the final knot in her leather cord. She sat on the hard floor blinking at her handiwork. Too tired to feel anything or even to try it out, she lay back against the warm hearth stones and drifted into an uneasy doze.

The door opened, startling her awake. From the light coming through the window, Echo knew she had not been asleep for more than an hour. Eirloch and his friends stood in the doorway.

"The deadline has arrived," Eirloch announced, his voice echoing in the room.

Jana moaned and pushed herself up into a sitting position. Her eyes were bright with fever.

"Echo?" she whispered. "I'm thirsty."

Echo hastened over and held a cup to her lips, but Jana lost interest and lay back down after a single sip. Echo stood and gestured at the finished chair.

"Here it is," she said. "I believe I have done what you asked, but please, I would like each of you to try sitting in it."

The fae entered the room and clustered around her contraption, their expressions skeptical. It did not look like much, Echo had to admit. Her stitching was nowhere near as neat and precise as Mamai's, but she had done the best she could, and leather was more difficult to manage than thread or yarn.

"What... is it?" the winged lion growled.

"A chair," Echo assured him.

"It... doesn't look like a chair," the white-haired girl said.

"I know," Echo said. "But it can't, can it? With the five of you all being such different shapes and sizes, any chair comfortable for one of you wouldn't work for the rest. We had to get a little creative, but I think you'll find this to your liking. Why don't you try it out?"

The guardians stared at it, their expressions skeptical.

"Oh, fine, I'll show you," Echo said. She climbed up onto the main part of the "chair." The furs conformed to her weight, but the sawdust and shavings within supported her as she wriggled herself into a comfortable sitting position. "See? It's perfectly safe."

She clambered out. "Now one of you try."

Each of the fae took a turn on the chair, and each of them nestled happily into the unusual seat.

"This is cheating!" the sable lion growled, his wings twitching.

"Why do you say that?" Echo asked, indignant at the accusation.

"Because," the fae creature spluttered, "you've done nothing more than... than... create a cushion!"

Echo crossed her arms and regarded him, attempting to emulate Jana's imperious stance. "Is it not comfortable? Is it not warm? Will it not keep you dry and out of the snow during the long hours of your duties as guard? Explain to me how this does not fulfill the requirements of the task you set before us."

The lion's lips pulled back, revealing sharp teeth. "I still say it's cheating. This is not a chair."

"But it's not exactly just a cushion, either," the white-haired girl said, settling herself into the seat once more.

"A large cushion," the lion admitted, "but still a cushion."

"I like it," the wolf said, draping itself over the upper portion of the chair around the girl's shoulders.

"It's a little tricky," the mole-man agreed, "like us."

An argument erupted between the four of them.

"Peace!" Eirloch shouted, his wings flaring to either side.

"Callen, I think you are outvoted. The rest of us like the chair."

"I didn't say I didn't like it," Callen sulked. "Just that she cheated."

"Well, when have we not appreciated that?" the wolf asked, pulling its lips back in a terrifying smile.

Callen's tail lashed. "Point."

Eirloch threw his head back and laughed, then he turned to Echo. "It's not often someone outwits us at our own game. Well done."

Echo's ears grew warm at the praise. "It was Jana's idea," she mumbled, staring at her blistered fingers.

"I'll confess that I did not believe you could do it," Eirloch said. He turned to his companions. "What do you say? Has she fulfilled our request?"

The others all nodded, and then one by one, they inclined their heads to Echo. Even Callen gave her a grudging nod.

"Then we shall guide them to their destination," Eirloch proclaimed. "Bring warm clothes for our new friends, for the journey is long and the snow is deep."

"My lady"—he raised Echo's fingers to his lips—"we will take you to the mortal gate. But we cannot pass through it alongside you."

"Taking us there will be enough," Echo said, tugging her hand out of his grasp and feeling suddenly quite shy.

At her discomfort, a grin flickered about his mouth and sparkled in his eyes. A few moments later, the guardians returned with bundles of clothes and furs and two pairs of tall boots in their arms.

"We leave as soon as you are ready," Eirloch said.

24

A WINTRY EXCURSION

The wind howled across the rolling hills. It flung glittering dust into the air like a trillion dancing fireflies. Echo held a mittened hand over her mouth and the tip of her nose, warming it with her breath. It never got this cold at home, but she had to admit, with her hands snug in a pair of heavy mittens, her feet protected by fur-lined boots, and the rest of her bundled in so many layers she could barely move, she scarcely felt the frigid temperatures as they hiked across the barren landscape. Ennis Rosliath did not get much snow, even in the winter, and Echo had never seen so much of it at once, so she gazed about in wide-eyed wonder at the way the snow sparkled in the sun like a field of diamonds.

At first, the wonder of their surroundings proved a delight. Even Jana had seemed to perk up as the crisp, fresh air washed over her. But as the hours wore on, trudging through drifts up to their knees and looking out at the barren, unchanging landscape, the initial delight faded. Echo's legs ached and she thought she could feel her eyes freezing over. Jana's newfound energy had dissipated; her head hung, and she neither looked up nor spoke.

Clouds tumbled across the sky and the wind whipped about them, intent on driving them back the way they had come. Every step became a struggle. Echo lowered her head to protect her face from the icy wind, but it seemed to drive at her from every direction at once and no matter which way she looked, stinging particles of ice found every patch of exposed skin.

With a low moan, Jana tripped and tumbled face-first into the snow. Echo scrambled over to her, floundering a bit as she hit a deeper patch. She knelt down next to her, lifting her off the ground.

"It's all right," Echo assured Jana, whose only acknowledgement was a long, slow blink. Echo pulled the other girl's arm around her shoulders and helped her stand. "How much farther?" she shouted after Eirloch.

He turned, saw their predicament, and retraced his steps, helping Echo support Jana. "Not far now," he shouted back. The wind seemed like a living thing, seizing his words and carrying them off over the frozen terrain. He pointed. "See that rise? It's just on the other side."

Echo nodded wearily. Together, the three of them continued to trudge through the snow. Thunder rumbled across the darkening sky, and Jana shuddered.

"What is that?" Echo yelled. She didn't think thunderstorms were normal for wintertime.

"The Winter King," Eirloch replied, his eyes wide.

"What?"

"That is his summons. Something must be wrong."

"Does he know about us?" Echo called, sudden fear quaking through her body. What if he knew she had trespassed into his domain and decided she would not escape again?

Eirloch shook his head. "No, that is his call to battle. One of the gates has come under attack!"

"From who?"

"Do I look like a soothsayer?" Eirloch shouted.

"I don't know!" Echo yelled, confused by his question and not sure what it had to do with anything. "Are you?"

"No! I wouldn't be a lowly guardian if I could see what was happening elsewhere!" Eirloch paused, his head turned in the direction from which the rumble had originated.

A new fear pricked at Echo's mind. "Do you need to answer the summons?" She dreaded his answer. But if the portal was as close as he said, she and Jana might be able to find it alone.

For a long moment, the young rifinn did not answer. Then he sighed. "No. I am to stay at my post. A second call would have meant all units."

Jana moaned and wilted. The sudden weight pulled Echo to her knees.

"Jana! Jana!" A surge of panic shot through Echo as she saw that the princess's eyes were closed. "We have to get her out of this cold. I have to…"

Eirloch nodded, his face grim. He lifted the princess in his arms as though she were a small child. "Come, you haven't much time." He began to stride away, his long legs carrying him quickly through the snow.

"What do you mean?" Echo asked, trotting after him. "I have a whole day left!"

Eirloch shook his head grimly. "The summer solstice has already begun."

"But... how... I thought..." Panic gave way to a rising hysteria as she realized how little time they had left.

"Time does not pass at the same speed across the realms, but the fae realms all revolve around the mortal world," Eirloch said, cutting off her stammering confusion. "And it doesn't take a soothsayer to know that the Summer Court are the only ones who would attempt to breach our borders. The only time they have the power for such an incursion is during the summer solstice."

Echo did not reply. She couldn't. It was taking all the breath she had simply to keep up with their guide's longer legs. Besides, anything she said at this moment might endanger her and Jana both. She sent a silent prayer of thanks to the Creator that the rifinn and his friends had asked so few questions about their unexpected guests.

They crested the rise and Echo paused, leaning on her knees as her lungs spasmed. It wasn't just the difficulty of hiking through the snow, however, that made her breath catch. The vista spread out before her was unlike anything she had ever seen. They had come to the edge of a sheer drop that plummeted down hundreds of feet. She had not realized they were already at such an altitude. Beyond the chasm before them, she could now see a majestic swath of mountains, their steely blue faces jutting up like jagged daggers from beneath the snow, their peaks hidden in the fog. But even as she looked, an opening in the clouds allowed the fiery rays of sunset to pierce the darkness, lighting up the snow-caps in a blaze of sparkling glory. Echo froze in place, her heart aching at the magnificence of it all.

"Come, it is not far, now," Eirloch said. He turned and strode along the ridge a few steps and then stopped at a place where the snow rose up in a mound. He brushed the powder away and Echo saw a large stone, similar to the pillar in the Celshike circle they had passed through but a few days before. This one looked older, its face weathered and dull. The runes etched around the sides appeared to have been ground away by years of standing unprotected from the elements.

"Here it is," he said. "I am truly sorry I cannot go with you, but if you both pass through the gate now, you will arrive in the mortal realm on the summer solstice as you wished. Though, I do not know what time of day you will find yourself in."

"Thank you for bringing us this far," Echo replied.

"You earned it." His face broke into a wide, amused grin. He eased Jana down and transferred her weight to Echo's shoulders. Then he stepped back and sketched a low bow, his outstretched wings a stark contrast to the desolate white land. "There are not many who can outwit the fae. You have my respect, my lady. And a promise: if your journey ever leads you back to Vetirheim, should you have need of me, only call my name, Eirlochian Ravensson, and I will come to your aid."

Echo swallowed past a sudden tightening of her throat. For a fae to give her its true name was no small thing. Even she, with her limited knowledge of their... well, her... kind, understood the power he had just bestowed on her. Yet, she knew he would not be so generous if he knew Jana's identity; her absence was the most likely cause of the attack on his lord's domain.

"I am honored," she managed. Echo stared at the ground, guarding her expression as best she could, grateful for the thick woolen scarf that hid most of her face. Jana's life depended on getting through this gate. Besides, he still had not displayed any remorse for kidnapping them in the first place, or requiring such a ridiculous task in exchange for his aid. Somehow, she knew the thought of an apology would never cross his mind. He was fae. In his mind, everything that had transpired was just and reasonable, even if it made no sense to her. And he had kept his word and done them no harm. Perhaps they were fortunate to have been discovered by Eirloch and not some other inhabitants of Vetirheim.

"You surprised me, little one. With your cleverness and determination, I believe you will go far, whatever realm you are in. Know that you have a friend in Vetirheim, should you ever return. Now, place your hand on the stone and it will allow you and your companion to pass through."

Still propping Jana up, Echo tugged off one mitten with her teeth and spread her palm against the stone. The icy shock of it burned her hand and shuddered down her arm, but the portal opened, and she and Jana tumbled through.

25

THE WELL

*T*he first thing Echo was aware of as she blinked her eyes in the darkness was the temperature. The air around her was far warmer than that which she had just left, but not as warm as she had expected. A dank mustiness greeted her nostrils and she breathed in cool, damp air.

The second thing she noticed was the wet. They were standing in water up to their knees. All around them, high walls rose up in a circle, and high above them, she could see a patch of light. She lowered Jana into the water and propped her up against a wall, then sloshed around, feeling along the walls with her hands. Hard, rocky clay crumbled away in her fingers and panic swept through her as she realized where they must be.

She sank down into the water next to Jana. The princess did not stir, and Echo had no hope of waking her.

"We're at the bottom of a well." The words dropped from her lips like stones atop a cairn. "The bottom of a well! Why would there be a door into Vetirheim down here? How are we supposed to get out?"

Her eyes began to adjust to the gloom and she looked around, a hopeless despair filling her. They had come all this way, but she could go no farther. There was no way to climb out, and even if she could, she could not carry Jana with her.

A faint, silvery glimmer on the opposite wall caught her eye. She stood and inspected it. The silver lines formed a rough rectangle like a door and Echo's spirits rose. This must be the door they had come through! As loath as she might be to return to Vetirheim, perhaps they could go back and tell Eirloch that he had made a mistake. She pressed her hand against the clay in the middle of the outline. The wall rippled and shimmered, and she thought she caught a glimpse of snowy vista through the door, but it was like peering through dirty glass. Echo put both hands against the portal, then she beat her fists against it and screamed Eirloch's true name, but the door remained firmly shut, and no help came.

Her gaze caught on the tendrils of roots sticking through the wall, and for one fierce eyeblink of hope her thoughts returned to the vines she had grown to get them out of the tower, but her mind immediately reeled back from the idea. Those had grown so fast, it was more likely that she would crush herself and Jana before they could climb out, and that was assuming Jana woke up. There was no way she could carry the unconscious girl up the vines quickly enough.

Sobbing, Echo fell to her knees, her forehead pressed against the unyielding wall. Her strength fled, her quest failed. Tears fell like raindrops into the water as she thought of all she had come through. For it to end here, so close to her goal, was intolerable, but she had run out of ideas. Hunger gnawed at the edges of her stomach, reminding her that she hadn't eaten anything since they left Eirloch's home that morning. Or was it yesterday? Time had become so confusing. All she knew was that it had been too long. She had consumed the last of her mother's carefully packed pastries in Eirloch's home. What she wouldn't give for a warm scone and some hot tea... Her mouth watered at the thought. She closed her eyes and summoned a memory of her mother's kitchen, warm and cozy and full of the aromas of good food.

She sniffled, wiping her nose on the back of her sleeve. The fingers of her other hand dug into the mud, conceiving a selfish, despicable notion that she could not help but heed.

Perhaps she could climb out on her own. Even if she could get Jana to the sea, perhaps it was already too late to save her. But it wasn't too late for Echo. If she could climb out, she could just go home. Her parents would be overjoyed to have her back. She would simply tell them she couldn't find their daughter, their true daughter, and they would believe that Echo had done her best. They did not know Jana. They just missed the idea of her, really. Her heart ached at the thought of leaving the other girl behind, but surely she was not required to die down here with her?

Quickly, Echo shed her extra layers and pulled off her new boots. Then, using her fingers and toes to dig into the earth, she began to climb. The clay was warm and sticky to the touch, and she found it easy to dig her feet into the saturated walls. However, the mud soon gave way to hard-packed dirt, and it became more difficult to create holds. The secret she carried with her weighed her down, making every movement twice as difficult. Drops of sweat rolled down her back and stung her wounds as she scratched and clawed at the well shaft, scrabbling her way up one inch at a time, the torn blisters on her hands protesting almost as loudly as the partially healed gashes in her feet. She had ascended about three times her own height when she reached an impassable stretch of slick, sheer rock. She reached, her hand searching for even the slightest outcropping to grasp, but there were none.

"No!" The scream erupted from her throat as her toes slipped and she plummeted, landing in the shallow water with a splash. Her legs crumpled beneath her, but the soft mud below the surface cushioned her fall, keeping her from injury.

Putting her face in her hands, Echo slumped over, completely spent. She had nothing left. Every struggle, every trial, every pain she had endured piled up on her shoulders and seemed intent on pushing her down into the murky muck at the bottom of this long-forgotten well. Her own selfishness fell upon her with even more crushing intensity, and she felt the shame of it carving its way into the depths of her being.

She dragged her weary body over to sit next to Jana. The princess's face was deathly pale, and her breath came in short, ragged gulps. Echo's chest constricted. Her sister was dying, and there was nothing she could do to save her. Wrapping her arms around Jana, she closed her eyes and buried her head in the other girl's shoulder. All she could do now was offer a modicum of comfort or warmth to her sister in her last hours.

"Creator," she whispered, "please take care of Mamai and Dadai. And forgive me for wanting to leave Jana behind, for thinking of her as a burden. And"—her voice dwindled to a nearly inaudible, despondent plea—"help me find a way to get us both out of here."

A soft fluttering sound reached her ears, and then she heard a plop as though something had fallen into the water.

Echo raised her head swiftly and pulled herself to her feet. Had someone happened by the well and dropped something in?

"Hello?" she shouted, her voice rasping. "Is someone up there? We're down here! Help! Please, we need your help!"

No answer came, though Echo continued to shout until her throat ached. At last, she gave up. Perhaps it had only been a squirrel dropping a nut, or even something the wind had carried along until it reached the mouth of the well. She turned back to Jana and collided with something hanging down from above.

Echo reached out and grasped it, her mind reeling as it scrambled to recognize what she held in her hands. A rope! Someone had dropped a rope! But then why hadn't they answered her calls? She frowned. Perhaps it had just fallen, or perhaps a gust of wind had dislodged the winch, though that seemed unlikely. She tugged on the cord and found it sturdy. A good length of it lay in the water; that must have been the sound she'd heard, though she couldn't figure out how she had missed it when she stood up. She measured it out and found that she had enough to tie a loose loop which she could slip over Jana's torso and tighten under her arms. If she could climb up the rope, she could use the winch at the top to pull Jana up. It wouldn't be the most comfortable trip for the princess, but it was better than dying at the bottom of this hole. She used her own furs to try to pad the rope a little more, and then tied the most secure knot her father had taught her.

She stared up at the rope, her mouth going a little dry at the prospect of such a long climb. Her palms and fingers were already complaining about the first attempt. But it was the only way out, and Echo was not about to squander this opportunity. Gritting her teeth, she wrapped her sore hands around the rope and hoisted herself up, digging her toes into the muddy wall of her prison and making the arduous ascent once more.

Hand over hand, she pulled herself up, using the foot-holds she had dug earlier until she reached the rocky bit. Taking a deep breath, Echo tightened her grip on the rope and tucked her knees up, then pushed her legs down, step-ping onto the rope with her right foot, bringing her left foot up underneath it and pinning the line between them. She moved her hands up the rope and repeated the motion. Over and over. One more move. One more. One more.

At long last, she reached the lip of the well and pulled herself up and over the short stone wall. The late afternoon sun beat down on her head and she wanted nothing more than to lie down and relish its warmth, but she was not yet finished. She stumbled over to the wheel and began turning it with what little strength she had left. Slowly, the crank turned the shaft and the rope began to wind in the winch, lifting Jana up from the bottom of that dark prison. When her head appeared above the stone wall, Echo set the brake on the wheel and reached out to grip great handfuls of the fur coat Jana was still wearing. With a mighty tug, she hauled the princess over the stones and onto the safety of solid ground where she lay, unmoving.

Working quickly, Echo loosed the rope and pulled the heavy clothing from her sister's unconscious form. Her chest rose and fell fitfully, but her eyes remained closed.

An owl hooted softly and Echo spun toward the sound as a large, winged figure swooped down over her head and landed atop the little roof of the well. She stared at the snowy-white feathers and the golden chevron on its shoulder. A wild thought struck her.

"Did you drop the rope?" she asked.

The owl gazed at her, his wise eyes wide and unblinking. Then, with a beat of his mighty wings, he lifted into the air and disappeared into the trees. Echo gazed after him, and then blinked, as though waking from a dream.

"I know where we are!" she exclaimed. "This is the old wishing well. But that means..." She shook Jana by the shoulder. "We're not far from my home! It's just a short walk down to the beach." She looked up; the sun hung low in the sky. "We have enough time. Jana! Jana! Can you hear me? I need you to wake up! I can't do this on my own, Jana!"

But Jana was hopelessly limp and unresponsive. Echo clenched her fists, resolve coalescing like quenching steel in her battered body.

"Creator, give me strength," she whispered.

Kneeling down, she put her hands under Jana's arms and began dragging her backwards, towards the edge of the Faeorn. Jana's dress trailed in the dirt, and the sodden pile of furs they left behind looked as forlorn as Echo felt. But she dug in her heels and heaved with all her might, struggling to pull her sister down the hill toward the crashing waves.

26

SUNSET

*E*cho's arms ached, and her spine felt like it was being crushed by a giant's fist. A clear fluid seeped from the raw blisters on her hands, and the wounds on both feet had reopened, first from the long climb, and now from shuffling backwards over rocks and pine cones and sharp thorns she could not avoid. She was doing her best not to jostle Jana too much, but she couldn't avoid every dip in the terrain. However, the girl's moans were encouraging if only because they meant she was still alive.

Sweat trickled down her back and dripped from her legs in the heat of summer's advent. Even this late in the day, the air was full of a humid warmth that enveloped her. Any other day, Echo might have been bothered by the oppressive mugginess, but now, so soon after her sojourn in Vetirheim, she couldn't help but marvel at just how great a privilege it was to be warm.

The sun continued to sink. Echo's heart raced, her breath coming in short gasps as she tugged Jana ever closer to the ocean. The roar of the waves filled her ears. The grassy ground suddenly gave way to sand under her bare feet, and she slipped, bringing them both tumbling down the dune. Scarlet streaks of her own blood stained the golden earth. She sat on the ground, panting. Carefully, she twisted her body and looked behind her. The ocean sparkled placidly, perhaps a dozen paces away. The surface rippled as little waves broke and curled over, their edges white and foamy above the deep, mysterious cerulean, like bony, grasping claws reaching up from the depths. It was the closest she had been to it in years. Her old fears assailed her with fresh vigor and she felt a strangling sensation around her throat.

"We made it," she whispered, her energy spent. "Jana! We made it! You... you need to..." Gently, she laid the girl's head down on the sand, then pulled the pack from her shoulder and upended it onto the sand, rifling desperately through its contents until her hands found the smooth pelt of the seal skin. She tugged it free and placed it over Jana.

Just as in the tower, nothing happened. Echo sat back, hoping that she just needed to wait. It would work, she told herself. It always worked in Dadai's books. Just at the last moment, always, something happened. Something came through.

"Creator," she cried, her voice still rasping and thin. "Please."

Jana's short hair stuck up in a tangled halo, full of leaves and twigs. Her clothes were tattered and damp and covered in mud. She looked nothing like a princess in this state, her skin clammy and deathly pale.

"Please, please." Echo wrung her hands. "I've brought you this far. But... the ocean... I can't. I can't go down there. Jana! Wake up! Creator, don't make me..."

But Jana did not stir.

"Maybe..." Echo lifted the selkie skin, a wild hope thundering in her ears between heartbeats. "Maybe you just need the water to touch you." Aching with every movement, she crawled a few inches closer to the water, dragging her wounded body to a nearby tide pool. Her muscles screamed at her, begging her to stop. Panting with the effort, she dunked the seal skin into the salty water, then crawled back up to the unconscious Jana and draped it across her once more.

Still, there was no response.

Far down the beach, the sun had just kissed the horizon.

"No!" Echo's voice grated painfully as she tried to scream. "No! Jana!" Clasping the unconscious girl to her, Echo's terror of the ocean abruptly suffocated beneath the fear of losing her sister, of Jana dying here on the sand, only a few feet from what would save her. She pulled frantically at her sister's shoulders, throwing herself against Jana's unconscious weight. But the last of her strength had gone, and even if she had, in the last moments, managed to overcome her fear of the sea, she could no more move Jana any closer to the ocean than she could grow scales and breathe fire.

Too weary to cry, Echo slumped to one side. Her vision blurred as hunger, exhaustion, and pain overwhelmed her. She had been so eager at the beginning, even arrogant in her belief that she could do this thing, bring back the daughter her parents had lost. It had been her secret wish to do this by herself. Though it had pained her to leave her father behind, hadn't her heart leapt at the opportunity to prove herself on this quest? What she wouldn't give to have his strength to lean on now! And Malilia—where had she gone? For days now, she had been expecting the elven woman to reappear, but she had not rejoined them as she had promised. She hoped nothing bad had happened to her. And Drayeth, the little fae-dragon who had helped convince Jana to come with her, who had gamely followed them out of the tower, and then disappeared after the Celshike gate. Where had he gone? She had not relished his help at the time, but what she wouldn't give to have it now!

Through the haze, she noticed two figures approaching. She tried to call out to them for help, but her voice was parched and shredded, and the breath that emerged carried no sound. The figures drew nearer and now Echo could make out that they were a man and a woman, headed straight for them at a run. She wondered where they were going in such a hurry. She tried again to call out to them, though she had no idea how to explain to them what she needed. Surely they would never understand; at worst, they would try to take them even farther from the sea. But she must take the chance, or Jana would die.

"Please, help me," she croaked.

Though it must have been nearly inaudible over the crashing waves, somehow, they seemed to hear her rasping plea. Then there was a rush of movement and two sets of arms were wrapping around her. At first, she thought they were trying to tear her away from Jana and she fought them off, or tried to; her feeble attempts were laughable at best. But then she heard her name being repeated and recognition broke through the haze that veiled her mind.

"Mamai? Dadai?" She tried to force her eyes to focus.

"We're here, Echo, darling, we've got you."

"Jana," she whispered. "We need to get her to the water."

"Dadai will carry her. Echo… you can let go now."

The words came to her as though across a great distance, and Echo squeezed her eyes shut against their assurances, her head throbbing in time with the rolling waves. She felt herself being lifted, and then a shock of cold snapped through her and she found herself standing waist-deep in water that stung her wounds with its salt. She panicked and clutched at Jana, who appeared to be floating on her back.

"Echo, let go." Mamai's voice was gentle but urgent. "She needs room for the transformation."

"But I tried that already, nothing happened!"

"Didn't I tell you she needed to be in the water? Gareth, hold her. She's delirious. I'll help Jana."

Strong arms clasped Echo about her shoulders, and she felt her hands being gently pried from their grip on Jana's arm. She tried to watch, but her eyes refused to focus. Mamai seemed to be holding Jana afloat with one hand and the seal skin with the other. A ripple of motion, the bobbing of a wave, and Jana disappeared under the water. Echo screamed and tried to dive after her, but something held her back. She tried to fight and ended up submerging her face, coming up spluttering and spitting sea water.

"Echo." Dadai's voice cut through her hysteria. "Echo, look."

An auburn-furred head emerged from the water and barked, sounding to Echo like joyful laughter. Mamai stood nearby, waist-deep in the water as the seal dove and circled her, its sleek body graceful as Jana danced through the waves.

"You did it, Echo," Dadai murmured. "My darling Echo, you brought her home."

Echo tried to speak, but blackness crept around the edges of her vision and she could no longer fight it back. Her eyelids fluttered closed.

27

HOME

*W*hen Echo came to herself again, she was snuggled down beneath something heavy and comforting, her body cradled in warmth. A silver light mingled with a fiery glow danced blearily beyond her eyelashes, and she thought perhaps there was something she ought to attend to. But beneath her stirring fingers was a familiar leafy pattern, sewn onto her quilt by Mamai many years ago, and before she could think any more, it had lulled her back into sleep. When she woke again, minutes or hours later, it was with memory, and the shock of it slammed into her with the driving force of a Vetirheim wind.

Her first thought was of Jana. She sat up from the couch in a sudden burst, her eyes darting wildly, hoping for some glimpse of the princess.

There!

Sitting in Mamai's rocking chair beneath a moonlit window, wrapped in blankets, her luminous hair dark with sea water, the Summer Princess sat with her eyes closed. Painfully, Echo tried to swing her legs over the edge of the couch, but her head spun at the sudden movement and she let out a loud groan.

"Echo!" The sweet, welcome voice reached her ears and then Mamai was there, wrapping her up in her arms. Echo buried her face in her mother's shoulder, drinking in all the familiar scents of brine, wild herbs, and baking bread, and felt all the pain and worry from the previous days begin to melt, ebbing away from the force of love in those arms. To be here, to be held, it filled her soul with a peace she had not known in many long, difficult days.

"I..." Echo started, then licked her chapped lips. "You found us."

"Yes. Praise the Creator, we found you." The tender ferocity of Mamai's embrace only intensified as she spoke. "It is good to have you home."

Home. How she had missed this place, her parents! How good it was to be safe and warm and protected. But her most pressing concern was not her own health or even the snug comfort of being home again.

"How did you find us?"

Mamai smiled gently. "It was the strangest thing. Shortly before sunset, Dadai and I were sitting down to dinner, not that we've had much appetite the past two weeks, when we heard a tapping at the window and saw an owl outside rapping its beak against the glass. It was so unexpected that Dadai stepped outside, and the owl took off, circling round and around him. I heard a shout and I ran outside to see that your father had followed the bird, which seemed to be guiding him to the cliffs. The bird then dove toward the beach and I screamed because I thought it was attacking your father, but then I heard him shout that someone was in trouble down on the shore. He raced down the stairs and I followed as fast as I could. You cannot imagine what we felt when we realized it was you."

"An owl," Echo breathed.

"A messenger straight from the Creator."

"Was it a white owl?" Echo asked, suddenly curious.

Mamai tilted her head to one side. "Why, I believe it was."

Echo felt a warmth spreading within her at the thought of the owl, her owl, and sent a whispered "thank you" flitting through the air. He had paid back her single act of kindness three times over. She glanced out the window, almost expecting to see him hovering outside, but of course, he wasn't there.

"Jana?" Echo asked, pulling herself back into the present and peering at her sister, still asleep in the rocking chair. "I thought she'd be better?"

Mamai's face grew radiant, and a faint smile touched Echo's lips as she basked in that smile, another part of home she had missed so desperately. "She is well," she assured her, nodding at the rocking chair. "Just tired. The transformation cured her, but when she returned to her human form she was exhausted and went right to sleep."

Echo nodded. "And Dadai?"

"He went outside to bring in Grainne from the pasture— much as he hated to leave us all, even for a moment." She chuckled, but it was hardly so much mirth as gratitude, over-flowing from her in laughter. "Ah, here he is now. Gareth," she called softly, "Echo's awake."

"Dadai!" Echo called out in a hoarse whisper.

"My wood-sprite!" Dadai crossed the room and lifted Echo from the couch in a tender embrace. She noted that he was careful of her back. "We feared the worst."

"I'm sorry for leaving you behind," Echo said when he set her down.

He raised a finger to his lips. "I ought to be angry with you, but I'm too happy to see you well and whole and to have you home. I want to hear everything."

With a sudden cry, Jana startled awake and looked around, blinking in the firelight. Echo saw the princess' eyes grow wide as her gaze darted between their faces. With a shudder, she pulled her legs up into the chair and wrapped her arms around herself as though attempting to make herself as small as possible.

"Jana." Echo slipped off the couch and nearly fell to the floor. Her legs wobbled, but her father caught her and helped her traverse the short distance so she could kneel at Jana's side. "It's all right," she soothed. "You're safe and well again."

Jana turned an uncertain gaze in Echo's direction. "I did not truly believe you when you told me your story," she admitted finally.

"Then why did you follow me?" Echo asked, confused.

A sad smile quirked at one corner of Jana's mouth. "Well, everyone thought I was dying. I believed them. Then you appear out of nowhere and tell me this preposterous tale about how my only hope is to follow you... well, I just figured what do I have to lose? And besides, it might be fun."

Echo coughed a disbelieving laugh and shook her head.

"But your words were true," Jana continued in a dull, life-less tone that was wholly unlike the sparkling enthusiasm Echo had come to associate with her sister's voice. "I am a selkie. I... I'm not even sure what that means. I was afraid of dying, but now I... I'm lost in a brand new world and I'm not sure what I'm supposed to do or where I'm supposed to go."

"I know that everything seems upside down right now,"

Echo said, taking Jana's hand in her own and giving it an encouraging squeeze. "But as for where you're supposed to go, you aren't going anywhere, because this is where you belong. We want you here. All of us want you right here."

Jana looked up, first at Echo, then at the adults standing around them. She shook her head. "I appreciate that, but... this is your home. I can't..."

"You can," Echo assured her. "This is your home, too. It's always had a place for you. A place that... was empty."

Jana sighed. "Thank you for the offer, Echo, but..." She broke off, staring more closely at Runa and Gareth. She rose, and took an unsteady step forward. "I..." She paused, shaking her head. "This... this will sound impossible, but... I know your faces." She reached out and took Mamai's hands in her own, gazing raptly up into her face, studying it wordlessly for long minutes. At length, she spoke, her voice quavering with unshed emotion. "You... you are the mother from my dreams."

Runa gave a hopeful, tear-stained smile.

"How is that possible?" Jana breathed. "How can I remember something from such a young age?"

"Selkie pups have a few advantages over human children," Mamai whispered, her voice sounding choked.

"You used to sing to me."

Mamai nodded. "Yes."

Jana turned to Dadai. "And you... your kindness, your laughter... fills my dreams, too."

Dadai chuckled, but his eyes glistened with tears.

Together, Mamai and Dadai reached out to envelop Jana. She leaned into their embrace, then reached over and pulled Echo in, as well.

When they broke apart, Echo sank down into a chair, her

strength fled. But she grinned happily up at Jana. "You're still the Summer Princess, you know."

"Not once my mo... the queen finds out what I am," Jana murmured.

Echo pursed her lips. "We can change her mind."

Jana gave a wistful sigh and gazed bleakly out the window. "You don't know her. She's..."

"Stubborn? Unyielding? Dauntless?" Echo suggested. "So are we. And we're stronger together."

Jana's lips twitched at that. "Sisters?"

Echo chuckled. "Sisters," she agreed.

Gareth laughed and pulled his wife close. "Runa," he said with an affected sigh as he regarded their two girls, "I'm afraid we have created a force to be reckoned with."

MENDING FENCES

The days of recovery were long. Echo's wounds were slow to heal, and it was a long time before she could walk without limping. The night after they returned home, she developed a high fever and spent several days in a state of hazy delirium. When the fever finally abated, Echo found herself weak and tired, with Mamai hovering anxiously about her and insisting that she stay in bed until she had healed completely.

Jana, however, was up and around within days, fully recovered and well-rested. Echo watched enviously from her enforced rest on the couch as Mamai taught Jana basic chores around the house.

The former princess did not complain about doing menial labor, though she held the broom in awkward hands and did not seem to understand the importance of lifting things from shelves to dust underneath them. Each day, they carried Echo out into the sunshine and let her sit in the yard wrapped in blankets for a time.

Gradually, life and strength returned to her, and Echo

found herself able to go on short walks down to the beach with Jana. Eventually, her hurts healed and her health improved enough for life to return to a semblance of normal.

"Mamai," Echo said one morning, "may I go down into the village?"

Mamai's brow furrowed. "What for?"

"There's... someone I need to see. Please, Mamai? It's important."

"Well," her mother drew the word out, "if you feel strong enough, I suppose there's no harm in it."

"I'm much better, Mamai." Echo forced a grin. "I even mucked out Grainne's stall this morning."

"Very well, but don't be gone long."

Echo turned to Jana. "Will you come with me? I want you to meet someone."

Jana nodded enthusiastically and the two girls left the house and made their way down the long, gentle slope of the promontory toward the village. Echo led them through the small row of houses until they came to the one she sought. She knocked on the door, nervous crickets doing a jig in her stomach. She was glad to have Jana there with her, standing at her side and reminding her to have courage.

A pretty woman with her hair bound up in a kerchief answered the door and peered out, her lips quirking into a perplexed line as she looked first at Echo, then at Jana.

Echo swallowed. "Is Branna home?"

Branna's mother nodded, wiping her hands on her apron. "Branna! You have visitors!" she called, disappearing from the doorway and back into the house.

A few minutes passed, and then Branna appeared, her footsteps slow and hesitant, her expression guarded. "Echo? I haven't seen you in weeks. I heard that you were ill..."

"Yes," Echo replied lamely.

"I'm sorry to hear that."

They stood facing one another, silence stretching between them. Echo shifted awkwardly from one foot to the other, trying to remember all her carefully thought-out words, but they fled from her mind.

Finally, Echo found her courage. "Branna, I wanted to come sooner, but Mamai wouldn't let me go far from the house until she was certain I was better. I have wanted to apologize for weeks." She looked up, directly into Branna's eyes, ignoring the heat of shame rising in her own cheeks. "I shouldn't have shouted at you and stormed off like that at our picnic. I thought you were mocking me, or setting up a prank for the others to laugh at me. I misjudged you, and I'm sorry, so very sorry for hurting you." Not knowing what else to do, she tugged on Jana's arm, pulling her up to stand next to her on the stoop. "This is Jana, my sister."

Branna's mouth dropped open slightly at this pronouncement. "Sister?"

Echo nodded. "It's a long story, but I'd like you to hear it. You played a part in it, actually." She gave a nervous little smile. "I hope... I hope you can forgive me. And... even more than that... I hope the three of us can be friends." The words were simple and stark and without decoration, but they expressed everything she'd wanted to say. The fear she had carried for so many years lifted from her heart, allowing the vulnerability of friendship to shine through. She suddenly felt weightless and free.

Branna's expression was unreadable as she stood in the doorway, her lips set in a thin line. Echo waited, her breath held in hope that desperately wanted to seek refuge in fear once again. The words she had so carefully constructed as she lay in bed these past weeks had abandoned her and the ones she had just voiced now echoed in her memory as pitiful, hollow things. Her heart sank as the silence continued, hot and oppressive around her. Whatever chance at friendship there might have been, she had killed it.

Then, suddenly, Branna let out a sob and hurled herself forward, throwing her arms around Echo and Jana. Echo stood, frozen for a moment, and then she embraced Branna back, and the three of them were all laughing and crying at once.

Finally, Branna pulled away, wiping her eyes on the corner of her apron. "Can I hear this story now?" she asked.

"Perhaps it is a good one to tell at a picnic," Jana suggested brightly. "What is a picnic, anyway?"

Branna's eyes widened and she turned to Echo with a questioning look.

Echo grinned. "Branna, would you be willing to help me show my sister the meaning of a picnic?"

Branna let out a laugh of delight, then drew herself up with a stern expression. "On one condition."

"What's that?"

"You bring some of your mother's scones!"

They all laughed.

29

AN UNEXPECTED REVELATION

*E*cho could not avoid the Faeorn forever. In spite of all she had suffered within Faerthain and Vetirheim, her spirit still tugged her toward the forest. She made daily excuses to herself for not going: Mamai and Dadai needed her help with something, Jana would be lonely without her, Grainne was off her feed and needed extra attention... but each day her excuses grew thinner until finally she was forced to admit that fear held her back. She spoke with Mamai about it.

"The forest is a part of your heritage," Mamai said, wrapping her arms around Echo. "You need it every bit as much as Jana needs the sea. But if you like, I can go with you."

Echo nodded into her mother's embrace. Together, they hiked to the outskirts of the Faeorn. An ominous pall hung over the forest in the heat of the summer sun. The trees loomed, their aspects forbidding and angry.

"I"—Echo gulped down tears—"I'm not welcome here."

A woman stepped out from between the trees. "Echo!"

"Malilia!" Echo smiled, then felt suddenly shy. "Mamai, I'd

like you to meet Malilia. She... well... she's my... um... she's my mother." Echo stumbled over the words, feeling awkward assigning that title to anyone but her own, dear Mamai. "She helped me find Jana," she added.

Runa smiled warmly at the elven woman. "You have my thanks."

Echo looked up at her mother. "May I..."

"Of course, my darling." Runa gave her an encouraging nudge. "I think we passed a patch of wild raspberries. That's just what we need for dinner tonight." She offered another gentle smile and then retreated back the way they had come.

Echo waited, feeling suddenly awkward and shy.

"Are you well?" Malilia asked. "I tried to find you. I am sorry I did not rejoin you at the tower like I promised. It was more difficult to get back than I had anticipated, and by the time I managed to return to Faerthain, you and Jana had already left. I intended to go searching for you, but then I received a summons from my queen. Drayeth saw you and the princess pass through the Celshike gate into Vetirheim and he went directly to Titania with the news. The king and queen summoned us all and we marched on King Ritioghra's door."

"We heard the call on the other side," Echo confirmed.

"The queen was furious when Ritioghra denied having abducted her daughter."

Echo shuddered, wrapping her arms around herself.

"She was even more furious when I finally told her the truth about Jana," Malilia continued.

A sudden premonition gripped Echo as she remembered Malilia's cryptic words about her father. "She... she didn't banish you?"

"No." Malilia's lips quirked oddly. "Actually, when her

anger passed, she seemed... forlorn, somehow. Perhaps one day..."

"Do you think she will attempt to reclaim Jana?"

"Not now that she knows Jana needs the sea. Queen Titania may be many things, but she truly does care for her daughter."

A silent shape swooped down from beneath the shadows of the trees and a snowy owl landed on Malilia's shoulder.

"You're out in the daytime a lot for a bird who's supposed to hunt at night," Echo commented wryly. "Not that I mind." She grinned at Malilia. "He saved my life. And Jana's."

"This is no ordinary bird," Malilia agreed, stroking the owl. "In many ways, he saved me, as well."

Echo frowned at her. "How?"

"Do you remember what I told you about your father?"

"You said he was a wood-elf and that he had been banished, but you wouldn't tell me why."

"Part wood-elf," Malilia said, then hesitated. "But also part human. A faeling, born in Faerthain. He was the first to speak out against Titania's abductions of mortal children. He was the first to shake my blind devotion to my queen. He was banished for daring to speak against Titania. I was furious with your father at the time and I tried to ignore the things he had said, but when you were born... all his arguments resounded over and over in my head, and when I looked at you, I couldn't help but agree with him." Malilia continued absently stroking the owl's snowy plumage. "The fae aren't all like me, or Titania," she said, as though speaking to herself. "Some of them are good and kind. Like your father. Even banished from his home and cursed to wear an unnatural form, he still manages to carry that kindness with him."

Echo's heart thudded in her chest as though someone had dropped something heavy on top of her. Her eyes widened as she looked at the owl and then back at Malilia. "Are you saying...?"

Malilia nodded, a sorrowful smile on her face.

Echo bit her lip, unsure of how to respond to such a revelation. The owl twisted his head and gazed solemnly at her, then hooted once, and with a flap of his great wings, lifted off Malilia's shoulder and disappeared back into the forest.

They watched him go, and Echo felt a strange sense of loss knotting in the pit of her stomach.

"I must go, as well," Malilia told her. "The queen has not banished me, but I am not in her good graces." She took one of Echo's hands between her own. "I just wanted to let you know how proud I am of you. The things you endured..." Malilia shook her head. "I know you may wish your heritage were otherwise. The fae are mistrusted in your world, and rightly so. But if there is any hope for my people, then I will cling to the fact that in you, an echo of what we could be, of what we might become, walks in the mortal realm."

With that, Malilia gave her a sorrowful little smile and then turned and also disappeared into the trees. A moment later, Mamai returned and stood next to her, an arm about her shoulders.

"Ready to go home?" she asked.

Echo of the Fae.

Echo raised her chin. The hated words no longer stung as they once had.

"Yes. I'm ready to go home."

30

ECHO OF THE FAE

"*H*urry up!" Jana urged, as Echo scrubbed, elbow-deep in the soapy water.

Echo grinned at her sister's reddened face and flicked a soap bubble at her. "If we don't do the chore right the first time, Dadai will just make us come back and do it over again," she said, rinsing the plate and setting it on the sideboard.

Jana huffed with impatience, but there was no true vexation in her expression. "You're right," she admitted, drying a bowl and placing it in the cupboard. "What story do you think he'll read tonight?" She clasped her hands together. "I hope he reads more about the good king."

Echo beamed. Jana had quickly fallen in love with the evening routine of listening to Dadai read to them before bed. Having a sister really was the best thing, Echo decided. It was fun having someone to get excited with—even if it was only about little things.

Finally, the dishes done, the two girls found their places on the couch. Mamai sat peacefully in her rocking chair, her fingers already busy with her knitting. Dadai laid the worn leather book across his lap. He grinned at them and then rubbed his knee.

"Storm tonight," he said, catching Mamai's eye. Then he began to read.

Echo's stomach lurched at the comment. It was the first storm since she had brought Jana home. The summer had been hot and dry, and Echo had managed to pretend for a while that her family was a normal, mortal family. Now, while her father read aloud, Echo's thoughts drifted out through the window to the surging sea. She could not focus on the story, her own tumultuous feelings rising in a surging tide, a foreshadowing of the storm to come. This was an experience she could not share with her mother the way Jana could. A sliver of bitterness wended its way around her soul, squeezing tight.

When he had finished reading, Jana and Echo each hugged their parents and then ascended the ladder to their shared loft. Downstairs, their parents blew out the lanterns and retreated to their own room.

Echo lay in the darkness, a mixture of emotions she could not begin to identify tumbling restlessly through her and keeping her from sleep.

"Echo," Jana's whisper sliced through the darkness. "Are you awake?"

"Yes," Echo whispered grumpily into her pillow.

"Will you come with me? Tonight?"

"What?" Shock coursed through her, followed by a paralyzing fear, and yet... the invitation quenched some of the fiery thoughts that had been erupting in her head.

"Mamai and I, we're going... out there... tonight." Jana gestured at the window. "The ocean... because of the storm.

I... I was wondering if you would come with us," Jana reiterated.

"I... why?" The question burst out of her lips more loudly than she intended.

A rustling sound, and then the silhouette of Jana's head popped up over the edge of Echo's bed from the mattress on the floor.

"Because I'm scared." Jana's soft voice whispered through the dark.

Something tight and bitter unwound in Echo's stomach at this confession. "Scared?"

"It's the first time I've gone in the ocean," Jana said. "Well, the first time I've been conscious, anyway. The last time is still kind of a blur, I was so sick... Mamai says it will feel as natural as breathing, but... the ocean is so big, Echo." Her voice squeaked and fell silent. "I just... I think I'd be braver if you were there."

"I don't know how much I can help," Echo whispered doubtfully, her own fear of the ocean foremost in her mind. "But if you want me to come, I'll come."

Some time later, thunder rumbled. Echo felt herself being shaken awake.

"Come on," Jana urged.

Stumbling out of bed and down the ladder, Echo joined Jana and Mamai and stood blinking in the dim lantern light.

"Echo?" Mamai's voice was surprised and... pleased?

"Yes," Echo mumbled, not quite all the way awake.

"Come, girls."

They followed Mamai out into the rain, across the yard and down the steps onto the beach. Waves tossed themselves heedlessly against the shore as the ocean rolled fretfully in its bed. Echo shuddered, wrapping her arms around herself, one eye warily on the dark water. In spite of the storm, there was little wind and the waves were not too rough.

"Are you all right?" Jana asked.

"I... yes," Echo replied, distracted by the hungry reaching of the water. "I... um... did I mention that I don't like the ocean much?"

A burst of lightning up in the clouds lit the ground and showed Jana's startled expression. "You don't?"

"No. It terrifies me."

"Oh!" Jana sounded dismayed. "I didn't think you... I didn't know... I'm sorry! I wouldn't have asked..."

"No," Echo forestalled her apology. "I wanted to come. I just... I don't know if I can go any farther."

"You don't think Mamai or I would let you drown, do you?" Jana asked. "I had hoped... I guess it was silly..."

Echo stared in disbelief at her sister's darkened form as rain dripped down her own face, sudden understanding dawning. "You wanted me"—her voice trembled despite her best efforts to control it—"to go out there"—she indicated the choppy sea with a wave of her arm—"with you?"

She could just barely make out Jana's timid nod. Laughter, wild and uncontainable, burbled up from deep within her and burst from Echo's mouth just as a rolling, booming rumble of thunder shook the night sky.

"All right," she exclaimed.

"Really?" Jana asked.

"Quick, before I start thinking straight again," Echo said.

Together, they raced down to the edge of the sea. Mamai stood there, the seal skins draped over one arm. She turned to them as they joined her and Echo imagined the expression of surprise her mother's face must hold to see both her daughters descending the beach. But Mamai said nothing, she merely handed Jana her skin and then, in a quick movement, Mamai stepped into her own skin and transformed. Echo could not have described exactly what happened. It wasn't so much that her mother put on the skin, as much as she melded into it, though it was hard to tell in the darkness.

The seal-form of their mother dove off the rocks into the water. The two girls watched her disappear under the waves. Echo felt a thrill of terror shudder through her until the sleek head popped back up above the surface.

"You don't have to do this," Jana said.

"I know."

Jana stepped into her own skin, transforming as effortlessly as Mamai. But when she was in her alternate form, she propped herself up on the rocks and looked at Echo, giving a short, inviting bark. Awkwardly, Echo clambered onto her sister's soft back, her arms and legs hugging the warm, sleek body of the seal. She closed her eyes and took a deep breath.

With a joyful bark, the seal slid into the sea.

Water covered her head, and Echo fought back the rising tide of panic, clinging to the seal with all her strength. It was all she could do not to scream. When they burst up through the waves once more, she took a long, gasping breath of air. Beneath her, the seal bobbed placidly on the rolling waves.

Echo looked wildly back to shore, amazed at how far they had traveled in such a short time.

"Don't let me fall," she whispered.

The seal shook its head back and forth in the water. Another seal joined them.

"Mamai?" Echo breathed.

The other seal barked and Echo laughed, her fears easing away. The storm was dying, the thunder growing more and more distant, the rain turning to a light mist. The sea itself stilled as the clouds above thinned to let silver rays of moonlight pass, bathing them in its gentle glow.

The ocean seemed more peaceful, out here, away from the shore. Echo slipped from the seal's back and tried a few experimental strokes, trying to keep up with her mother and sister. One of the seals flapped a fin, sending a spray of water at her face. Echo shouted and splashed back. The three of them circled and dived and splashed for a while, until Echo grew tired. Then one of the seals, the smaller one, ducked under her and buoyed her up on its back once more.

Echo gazed off at the dark horizon and smiled. "Let's go see what's out there," she whispered.

The two seals barked in agreement while Echo laid her head down on the soft back, surprisingly content in this newfound freedom. Then she sat up, raising her arms triumphantly to the sky.

"I am Echo of the Fae!" she announced to the night. "The girl who swims with selkies." She grinned.

Behind them, a little house on a promontory of land waited, a lantern in the window. They would return before dawn, slipping quietly through the misty gray light, back to the home they all loved. They would talk and laugh and tell stories. There would be good food to eat and warmth in the hearth. Land and sea. For the first time, Echo could understand how her mother could love both so equally.

When they got home, Dadai would be there, a smile on his face, his arms ready to embrace them all. Perhaps, on the next stormy night, Echo would be able to persuade him to join them. But for tonight, it was just his three girls, dipping through the vast ocean, the horizon their only boundary.

ACKNOWLEDGMENTS

Writing a book is always a group effort for me. There are so many people to thank, and I'm always worried I'll forget someone important, because everyone who pours into me and helps with my books is extremely important.

This particular book is what "they" refer to as a "heart project." I didn't exactly intend to write it, but it's one that the Lord laid on my heart rather firmly. I'd like to thank my Lord and Savior, Jesus Christ, for giving me the talent and desire to write stories, and particularly for giving me this story and helping me every step of the way.

I'd be remiss if I did not mention my incredibly supportive family: my husband, for encouraging me to lay aside my other projects and focus on this one, for reading part of an early draft and for continually brainstorming with me and giving me someone to bounce ideas off of. My dad, for being my first reader and content editor and for not being afraid to tell me that I hadn't quite stuck the landing, and for working diligently with me through twelve versions of the ending until we finally found the perfect recipe! My mom, for being my last reader and proofreader, helping me make sure that everything is as polished as possible before handing it to my readers.

I need to thank my earliest beta readers and target-audience testers: Lydia, Leiana, and Nathalie, for your help with ideas on the title and feedback on the story in general. Also, many thanks to H.L. Burke, Martha Rasmussen, Sarah Ashwood Blackwell, Georgina Bradford, Rosanna Gray, and Heidi Skinner for your valuable feedback throughout the early stages of this story.

Much thanks to the local coffee shop, whose Scone of the Day gave me the idea for Mamai's baking skills. Dear Reader, if you're ever in Chippewa Falls, WI, I highly recommend you swing through Bridgestreet Brew and grab a pastry!

To Ally, thank you for being ruthless. I know you may worry, but I truly appreciate your willingness to tell me where things need to be improved or point out where I've overused words or phrases or where the pacing needs work or plot holes and inconsistencies! And I love that you're willing to chat with me on the phone and brainstorm ways to fix things and that you always give me synonym options. I also appreciate you sprinkling in words of encouragement in an effort to remind me that you actually do like my stories. Working with you always makes me a better writer. But more than that, you are a dear friend.

To Deborah, thank you for fitting me in at the last minute

and being another set of eyes on my manuscript and catching all my typos and punctuation errors!

To my Book Dragons, for your enthusiasm throughout the writing of this story, for your encouraging words, for your excitement as I posted snippets, and for your incredible patience, you are all so very dear. Thank you for walking through this process with me.

And finally, to the young cashier who graciously let me use her name for this story, thank you! I don't know if I'll ever be able to get a copy of this book into your hands, but I hope you read it someday.

ABOUT THE AUTHOR

Jenelle first fell in love with stories through her father's voice reading books aloud each night. A relentless opener-of-doors in hopes of someday finding a passage to Narnia, it was only natural that she soon began making up fantastical realms of her own. Jenelle currently resides in the wintry tundra of Wisconsin—which she maintains is almost as good as Narnia—with her knight-in-shining armor and their four hobbits. When she is not writing, she homeschools said hobbits and helps them along on their daily adventures... which she says makes her a wizard.

www.jenelleschmidt.com